AF512483

THE LAST MESSAGE: THE LOST MESSAGE

DIPAVALI SEN

Invincible Publishers

First published in India in 2018

©2018 Dipavali Sen, All Rights Reserved

ISBN: 978-93-87328-83-9

No part of this publication may be reproduced or stored in a retrieval system, or transmitted in any form or by any means, electronic, mechanical, photocopying, recording or otherwise, without the prior permission of the publishers.

Invincible Publishers

G-120, Sushant Lok III, Sector 57, Gurgaon-122002

Registered Address: Opposite Kasturba Ashram,
Radaur, Haryana - 135133

Cover Design: Ashish Samant
Printed at Thomson Press (India) LTD

To
those who love living in the countryside and learning from the past,
those who believe in the forces of Nature and the courses of History,
like
my late father
Dr M.K.Sen, Professor, English, Burdwan University, had done.

Acknowledgements

I would like to express my gratitude to the staff of Invincible Publishers for all the work on this book. I would also like to thank Sri Guru Gobind Singh College of Commerce, Delhi University, for providing me the opportunity to teach papers on Economic History of India and Indian Economy. I gratefully recollect my youthful years in the districts of Birbhum and Bardhaman in West Bengal.

Contents

CHAPTER 1

1

Ratna in Shalboni

"I am sure the gold and the jewels are buried underground," said Ratna, "and I am sure we will find them. We must!"

"Yes! I am sure we will," came the reply. "I have resolved to leave no stone unturned, quite literally."

"Ooh! Neel-dada, let me help you. I am sure I can be of some help."

"Of course! Why not! Ratna, your very name means `*ratna*' or gem, but I have this project under control," grinned Neel, "at least for now."

Ratna drew in a lungful of the air that blew over the paddy fields of Shalboni (a village near Shal Forest). "Such fresh air! Such green fields!"

"That is because I do not use chemicals in my field or farm," declared Neel proudly, "I use completely Organic methods of farming."

Fourteen-year-old Ratna nodded in agreement. In the last few days, she had heard this term a little too many times from her nineteen-year-old cousin, Neelesh Chowdhuri.

Ratna lived in Delhi, the vast busy city that was the capital of India. Her father owned a tenth-floor suite in a high-rise building.

Currently, she was visiting her ancestral village of Shalboni near the Bengal-Bihar border with her parents. As she walked back from the paddy field with Neel-dada, Ratna could see the mansion that was their family home.

"Chowdhuri Niwas," it said in raised cement lettering on the front gate. The Abode of the Chowdhuris. An old and stately mansion, somewhat in need of repairs, and very different from the smaller buildings that clustered beyond it. Some of those buildings were earthen, with roofs of tin, tiles, or even thatch. Some were made of bricks and washed over with pink and green paint. But the mansion towered over all of them. *Jomidar-bari* (the landlord's house) as it was still called, was a *pucca* house of brick and mortar, even marble!

Ratna's great-grandparents had built it in the late 19th century, around the year 1860. It had an outer wing (*baar mahal*), the *kachhari* (court), and an inner wing (*andar mahal)*. The *kachhari* was where the villagers used to go and meet the landlord to pay their dues or make their pleas for help. The *andar mahal* was where *Jomidar-babu* and his family lived, where village women often went to cook and clean and generally serve the ladies of the landlord's family. There was also a *thakur-dalan* or pavilion where the Durga-puja was held every year. The building was stately but old. Here and there *Pipul* shrubs poked their heads out of the brickwork. An old *palki* (palanquin) that the earlier landlords had used as their mode of transport lay outside, idle and empty, gathering dust and bird droppings. Beside it stood, ramshackle but running, the car used by the present generation.

There were fruit gardens around the mansion, and a big pond overgrown with *kachuri-pana* or water-hyacinth. Both the pond and the fruit gardens had been out of bounds for the villagers, but the village kids often used to creep into the gardens and pluck fruits like *aam- jaam- kantthal* (mango, jamun, and jackfruit), or to fish in the pond for the *Ruhi* fish that were then bred there.

It was but a hole now, all choked up with hyacinth. The mauve flowers were pretty but they grew so fast that they left only patches of water for the villagers to use.

On the other bank of the pond, that is, opposite to the mansion, stood a recently build brick shed. It was used as a village store that sold daily provisions. It was owned by the moneylender-turned-merchant of the village.

The paddy fields were all around the village and the railway station was located even beyond, very close to the field that was adjoined to river named Jaltungi. This was a tributary of the great river Damodar, from which the DVC (Damodar Valley Corporation) derived its name. Evenings were ushered into the village with the howling of foxes from the riverbank, forested with Shal trees but deserted.

"Come, let's hurry," said Neel, "Ma must be ready with our lunch."

Ratna hurried along towards the mansion.

Entering the mansion, she made her way to the old-fashioned kitchen. She walked through the spacious drawing room, the corridors and courtyards. The entire floor was carpeted, although patches of marble were showing through in some places.

There were ornate and old-fashioned sofas and couches, along with low marble-topped tables in the drawing room. Oil-paintings hung down from the walls, where the discoloured white-wash was chipping off. There was a big black landline telephone on the side-table; it had brass decorations and decorative numbering. There were marble statuettes in the Greek mould as well as brass, Terracotta and Dokra icons.

The corridor had old-fashioned lanterns fixed to the walls. The courtyard was sunny and open; it led to a huge somewhat dark kitchen and larder.

While Ratna's father, Somesh Chowdhuri, lived in Delhi with his family, her father's elder brother, her Jetha or Uncle, lived in this ancestral mansion. `Jethi-ma' (Elder Mother)' was what Ratna called her aunt, Neel's mother. She wore *sari*s all the time and always had a vermilion dot on her forehead.

Ratna found her to be still in the process of readying the family lunch.

"Come, Ratna, sit by my side. Here is some *halud* (turmeric)," said Jethi-Ma, "make a paste for me. Khiri –our maid – is late." "Turmeric paste! But- but- I don't know how to make it!"

"Learn then. At your age, I knew such things."

Ratna sat beside her aunt and, according to her instructions, began to make the paste upon a big slab of pock-marked stone.

At the same time, she wondered where the family valuables could be hidden. Could they be hidden in the courtyard somewhere, the corridor or the kitchen itself?

Well, as Neel-dada had said, they must look everywhere and leave no stone unturned. Perhaps the very slab of stone upon which she was making this turmeric paste was the cover for a trap-door to a treasury that lay below the kitchen. Ratna moved the slab a little but found there was nothing but solid floor below. Well, well, no harm in trying, she told herself. That was the only way she could help in the recovery of the family fortunes. Meanwhile, her aunt chatted with her.

"It's a good thing that Somesh *Thakur-po* (Brother-in-law Somesh, that is, Ratna's father or Baba as Ratna called him) decided to come here this time. Your Jetha (that is, her husband) needs to sit down with him and discuss the sale of the house. Is it the right thing to do or not? Arre, arre, don't come down with such force upon the turmeric. You will crush your fingers. Now, as I was saying, your Jetha needs to discuss the sale of the house with your Baba."

Ratna knew that this was indeed the reason why Baba had taken leave and had come to Shalboni.

It was not so much a matter of dividing up the sale proceeds but to whether to go forward with the sale. They had recently received an offer but was it to be accepted?

"Your Jetha and I would, of course, like to stay here especially since Neel has decided to go into farming. But your father has his job in Delhi, and your mother is such a "*Dilliwali*". Born and brought up in Delhi, and teaching at a Delhi college! And you! You have years of schooling left there in that public school of yours. I see no chance of your coming back here. Perhaps it is better that we dispose of the whole thing and divide up the money. There, put a few drops of water now on the paste before you go on."

"Jethi-Ma, if the house is sold, where will you stay?"

"Oh, with the money we get we will build a small house here itself. A house which is light and airy and has all the modern facilities."

"Jethi-Ma, don't you like it in this house?"

"Enough of turmeric. Now take some *ada* (ginger) and grind it."

"Jethi-Ma, don't you like it here?"

"I would have loved it here," said Jethi-Ma, "had there been enough money. It is cracking and breaking and sinking and melting and we can't get it repaired or painted. It is almost in ruins now and that hurts me."

She wiped a tear and added, "Better to dispose of it."

"Who has made an offer for it, Jethi-Ma? Someone from Shalboni?"

Jethi-Ma seemed a little irritated at this. "Who in this village would have the money to make an offer for the house? Well, the *mahajan* (moneylender) might, but would he have the nerve to make us – the erstwhile *jomidar*s – an offer?"

But someone *has* made an offer, thought Ratna. A concrete offer that made Baba come here to give the matter a serious consideration. The two brothers would put their heads together and come to a decision.

Maybe the property would be sold.

All the more reason why the valuables hidden in it had to be found quickly. For, if the property gets sold, they would get sold with it.

Neel-dada had written to her that they just could not let this happen.

"Will this much ginger paste do, Jethi-Ma?" Ratna asked, feeling a little tired of the activity.

Ma too came in, smelling of sandalwood after her bath.

"Didi (Elder Sister), let me help you. Ratna, go and get the mixer-grinder from my room. I unpacked it but forgot to get it down. If it works, then Didi, you won't have to squat on the floor and use the grinding stone."

Ratna rose and went into the small courtyard. Salted and grated ginger lay drying in the sun there, along with pickles of all sorts. Then came the staircase, winding up to the bedrooms. For the visit, one of them had been given to Baba and Ma, and one to Ratna. A room all to herself, with ornate doors and windows. One of the doors was closed on the other side. The other was atop the staircase.

Yes, Ma had unpacked the mixer-grinder she had brought from Delhi. It was by the side of her bed, which was a big teakwood affair.

Ratna got it down to the kitchen and helped in connecting it to the archaic switchboard. But once it began to work, she went out – not only out of the kitchen but out of the *andar-mahal* (inner apartments) itself.

Swirling in her head was the thought of the family treasure, the gems and the gold, all hidden somewhere. Wouldn't it be wonderful to find them?

2

In the Old Kachhari

Wandering by herself, Ratna entered another part of the mansion, the *baar mahal* that led to the old *kachhari*

The *kachhari* had black-and-white marble squares as flooring, several doors with arches above covered in coloured glasses, chandeliers, and a huge couch with its curved legs ending in claws. Everything was covered in a sheet of dust. Above, in the ceilings, pigeons cooed as though they were surprised to see her. "How was it in the old times?" Ratna wondered and suddenly found the room full of people.

An elderly man with fine features and in fine silk lay among cushions of various sizes and shapes. He looked tired and weak. A hawk-nosed man in a turban sat beside him on a lower chair. He too was an old man.

The entrance of the hall was crowded with village folk and *lathiyal*s or guards wielding sticks. The turbaned man called out their names. One by one they came up with folded palms to the couch.

"Gupi-mohan!"

"I beg of you, *Jomidar*-babu, give me some more time to repay you," begged the man. "My wife was ill and I have spent all my money on her treatment."

Jomidar-babu was chewing a fragrant *paan* (betel leaf). His eyes glowed red.

"Nayeb-moshai, what do you say?" he asked the man sitting beside him, addressing him with a degree of respect that the term *moshai* (a colloquial form of *mahashay*) carried. Nayeb-moshai whispered into Ramesh-babu's ear.

"Well, Gupi," Ramesh-babu nodded and then drawled on, "If you don't have the money to repay me just now, plough my land for free till you can."

"For free, babu? What will I feed my family then? How will I get my wife treated?"

"That's your lookout," shouted Nayeb-moshai, and called another name. "Razak Mian, what about your dues?"

A bone-thin man fell at the feet of the man on the couch. "You know how there was a drought recently? *Jomidar*-babu, I cannot pay you this year."

"You did not pay last year as well. Forfeit your land", ordered Nayeb-moshai.

Razak began to wail, but Nayeb-moshai called out another name.

"Shyamu!"

A boy around eleven or twelve was hauled up by a guard with a big bamboo stick. It turned out that yesterday he had been caught fishing in the landlord's pond, which was closed to the rest of the village. Although he had hidden among the bushes in a shady corner, Haru *lathiyal* – the guard with the stick–had caught him and locked him all night in a shed and had brought him to court this morning.

But suddenly the boy gave one tug on his hand and freed himself. He then dashed across the hall, made his way through the men who stood outside and ran out.

In a second the whole scene seemed to shake and break into a thousand pieces and then fly away.

Ratna found herself in the empty hall, with dust all around and pigeons cooing above.

She felt as if she was choking and quickly went out.

3

Neel on Jomidari

Ah, there came Neel-dada. He had a shock of curls on his head, a sunny smile, always in *kurta-pajama* and a *jhola*.

Who would say that he had been to the United States last year!

He was lugging an assortment of vegetables in the *jhola*. Brinjals, carrots, potatoes, gourd, tomatoes, and a lot of coriander leaves.

"All from my experimental organic farmland," he said proudly. "Don't they look colourful?"

"Neel-dada, tell me something. Are *jomidar*s still around? And *nayeb*s? Our Social Science text mentions that they are a thing of the past."

"Of course they are gone. Why, what a question!"

"But I just saw —-", Ratna stopped herself. Neel-dada was likely to laugh if she told him that she had just been in a *jomidar*'s *kachhari* just now.

Instead, she said, "What I really wanted to know was how did they go and when."

"You didn't quite ask that you know. Anyway, before I tell you how and when they went, let me tell you how and when they came, rather, were brought into India's agricultural system."

They had come up to the hyacinth-covered pond now. Neel sat under a thick jackfruit tree. Ratna chose to sit under a shady Jamun tree.

"Who is a *jomida*r?" said Neel. "*Jomi* or *zamin* as it is called in northern parts of India means `land'. Jomidar or Zamindar means the landlord. Now, `Lord' in what sense?"

Ratna listened, smiling inwardly at how like a professor Neel spoke.

"In 1757 the British, rather, the British East India Company, fought with the Indians in the field of Palashi which they pronounced as Plassey. The British won the Battle of Plassey and that for the first time became the owners of some land in Bengal and, therefore, India. They gradually increased this control and in 1793 passed a law known as the Permanent Settlement Act. Or, as we call it, *Chirasthayi Bandovast*. This was the doing of one Lord Cornwallis, Governor-General of India during 1786-95.

Under it, some villages, that is, some land areas were put in charge of specific people who became known as Zamindars or landlords of those villages or areas. With the help of their *Nayeb*s or *Gumashta*s, that is, accountant -cum-advisors, they would collect taxes from the people of the villages under them, and provide a certain amount fixed as per the Act by a certain date every year to the local British Magistrate or Collector. Thus, they came in between the owner of the land, the East India Company, and the actual tillers–the people of Bengal. The *Jomidars* or *Zamindar*s were – to use the correct term–`intermediaries'."

"And the Permanent Settlement?" asked Ratna, "What does it mean?"

"It meant that the amount that the landlord had to give to the British collector was settled or decided permanently and forever. If he got more from the villagers, that margin or extra would be his. He could use it to improve the way his lands were cultivated and so increase their yield. That would benefit him as well as the people who were in his *jomidari*.

But if he failed to reach the amount to the British authorities within the due date, he would lose the *jomidari*. The office would go to someone else.

If no such thing happened, he would hold the position forever and so would his son and grandson. *Jomidari* was hereditary – as long as the British officers got the settled amount.

That gave the *jomidar* a lot of power over his area, such as judging village disputes and keeping *lathiyal*s or armed guards to protect his property.

Even after 1857, when the people of India rose against the East India Company and 1858 when Queen Victoria took the country into her hands, the same system continued.

This would not have been so bad if the *jomidars* had ploughed part of their margins into the land and raised its yield.

But most of the landlords took no interest in improving the way cultivation was done in their areas. They assigned even the work of tax collection to underlings – the *Nayeb*s and *Gumashta*s–and moved away to cities like Kolkata and Patna. They frittered their money in lives of luxury. The land and the people suffered. Crop yield stagnated or even fell. Then there were the natural calamities. In case of droughts and the floods, or locusts destroying crops, the farmers got little or no mercy. For, the *jomidar* stood to lose in that case – lose his entire *Jomidari*. So, even under Queen Victoria and the kings who followed, village India continued to suffer."

"But there was the freedom struggle and the British went away in 1947," Ratna broke in.

"Yes, Ratna," said Neel, "once India was independent, property and tax laws began to change. Various state governments passed laws for the Abolition of Intermediaries which is what the *jomidar*s had been. In 1952, Rajasthan did it. In 1955, West Bengal. The very title Jomidar was gone with the West Bengal Land Reforms Act of 1955."

Ratna asked: "Did it mean that since then that *Jomidar-babu*s were no longer to be called *Jomidar-babu*s?"

"Yes," smiled Neel, "Such titles became defunct. The landlords lost their titles and their positions. They still retained much of their land and influence but it was not the same."

A few purple *jamun*s – late ones because summer was at its end – fell onto Ratna's lap.

Neel stretched out his hand for them.

" They are unwashed!" Ratna exclaimed.

"Don't be so finicky," laughed Neel as he popped some into his mouth.

"Neel-dada, was our great grandfather a *jomidar*?"

"Yes, his name was Ramesh. He had a son named Suresh, and the *jomidari* would have come to him after

Ramesh if it hadn't been abolished. This Suresh was our grandfather. So if the system had continued, Baba and Kaka – my father Dwijesh and your father Somesh – would both have inherited half of the *jomidari* each. That was the rule. *Jomidari* was hereditary unless it was forfeited by non-payment of dues to the collector."

"What happened if the *jomidar* had many children – like it used to be in those times?"

"The children would all get shares, I mean, the boys. It used to be common that someone was a *jomidar* all right but only of 25 per cent of the *jomidari*. He would pay only one-fourth of the dues fixed by the Permanent Settlement, collected out the villages – the one-fourth – that had fallen to his lot. People used to taunt them as `*char ana r jomidar*. (one-fourth of a landlord)'.

The mid-day sun shimmered on the centre of the pond in the places that the hyacinth had not completely covered. Ratna felt hungry.

But she asked one more question, "Neel-dada, aren't you sad–just a wee bit sad -that you will never be a `Jomidar-babu' like our forefathers had been?"

"Not everybody wants to cling to the past," the answer was prompt, "the power and the position. No, that does not bother me. But do I wish I could find the accumulated wealth of the *jomidari* that is lying hidden somewhere!"

""Where do you think it could be?" asked Ratna as the two of them went back for lunch, "Any clues? Any hints?"

"Well, there's a message ... the last message ... but it is lost."

That is all she could get out of Neel just then.

CHAPTER 2

4

Meeting Mita

Next morning Baba took Ratna to see an old friend in the village.

It was a small house with no plastering over the brickwork. But the man seemed to be overjoyed to see Baba.

"After so many years! Somesh, you still remember us!"

"Bhupen, how can I forget you? We went to the *pathshala* (village primary school) together!"

His wife offered them homemade sweets and his daughter Mita brought them water in shining brassware glasses.

In a corner of the room stood a plastic can of pesticide. Bhupen pointed to it proudly.

"It is new stuff, said to be even more powerful than those introduced at the time of the Green Revolution in the mid-sixties in Punjab and Haryana."

"Is it so? But remember, nowadays people are complaining about the use of chemical fertilizers. My own nephew – Neel – is totally against it."

"Well, I have got the stuff and had even borrowed money to do so", Bhupen said, "as well as put up with a lot of insults from the *mahajan* (money-lender), that Vishnu Poddar fellow. He went on and on about how I still owed him money."

"But it was because the crops failed and we had no money to pay him," said his wife. "Did you tell Vishnu *mahajan* that?"

"As if he didn't know about the drought!" Bhupen said bitterly.

"Anyway, why bore Somesh-babu about all our sufferings. Somesh-babu, tell us about life in Delhi," said his wife.

Mita and Ratna, who were about the same age, became friends. They chatted about this and that and found that though they lived differently, they had a lot in common.

Mita had eyes bordered with *kajal*, oiled hair in plaits and was in too long a skirt. She wore glass bangles on her wrists.

She knew who Neel-dada was although she had not spoken to him much. Dwijesh Chowdhuri, though not a *jomidar*, was still a very prominent person in the neighbourhood and young Neelesh Chowdhuri was his son.

"Once Neelesh-da had come to our school, asking for help in cleaning the village pond. Some of us wanted to help but the teachers were not too keen. So, it did not happen."

Later in the evening, Ratna asked Neel about this. "Yes, don't you see how the pond is choked with hyacinth and garbage. It should be cleaned," he lowered his voice and continued, "Perhaps the wealth lies buried at its bottom."

"What makes you think so, Neel-dada?" Ratna's eyes shone on hearing this.

"Well, some lines that Ramesh Chowdhuri – the last *jomidar*–left on his deathbed, as a message."

"What lines? Where were they?" Ratna said she couldn't stop jumping on hearing this.

"That's the problem. The lines are lost."

"Lost! How did that happen?"

"Well, it did. The dying man was unable to speak, but he tore a page from his diary and gave it to his son, Suresh, that is, our grandfather. Suresh cast his eyes upon the lines on the torn page. But he was so distraught that he flung it aside and tended to his father. Once the last rites had been performed, he looked around for the paper but could not find it. He searched high and low, but the torn page was gone. All he remembered were its first and last lines–*Matir bhitor ratan anek "* and "*jodi bhasao jale"*. "This was the last message that Ramesh Chowdhuri gave to his son who lost it!"

" Oh, Neel-dada. We must lay our hands on those buried gems and gold!"

"Yes, but I don't know where to begin. I thought the village pond could be a starting point. It is a waterhole in the dry land of Birbhum with a connection- somewhere deep down–with the river Jaltungi. It was deepened and widened by the landlord's men. "If on dry earth you let water flow?".....Doesn't it connect to the rhyme? It could have been easy to bury things there since in Ramesh Chowdhuri's time the pond was exclusively for the *jomidar* family. Common village folk were not allowed to use it."

"Why did you go to the school, Neel-dada? Mita was telling me that you did."

Neel looked at the horizon. They were standing on a balcony of the mansion. All around them they could see the village and the field.

"I don't have the money to hire labourers to do the job and I don't want to bother Baba about it. So I tried to see if the school-children could help under the tag of doing a social service project."

"Why don't we try ourselves? Just you and I and perhaps Mita and any other who may wish to join?"

"Don't let anyone else into our secret," Neel instructed.

"But that way we will always be all by ourselves", said Ratna. "I'll tell Mita just enough to make her join us."

She did and found that Mita was already aware that there may be buried treasure under the pond. "Everyone in the village knows it but nobody is bothered to really look."

5

The Vishnu Stores

A couple of days later, early in the morning, Neel, Ratna, Mita, and a neighbourhood kid named Binu went up to the village pond next to the mansion, almost rising from it as it were.

The village provision store stood on the opposite side. Once that piece of land had also belonged to the Chowdhuri family, but it had been sold off when some years earlier the family had needed cash. The village moneylender, Vishnu Poddar, had bought it and set up a provision shop there–the 'Vishnu Stores'. He had not bothered about cleaning the pond or its banks.

They began to pluck the water-hyacinths, and lift them up. Sweat began to pour from their bodies as they worked. By mid-day, they had managed to do little. They were already tired out.

But next morning they were back again, with some more village kids. A few curious parents too came along.

"It is unhygienic to have hyacinth choking up the village pond," Neel explained, "so we – the young people of the village – are cleaning it ourselves."

A few were so impressed at Neel's talk that they too joined in the digging. The task was backbreaking but they were back the next day. And the next. Within a week, the pond was clear of hyacinth. The stinking pile was not immediately removed but lay in a heap by the side of the pond that was towards the mansion.

"Let it dry and then we will burn it", declared Neel.

Jethi-Ma was pleased. "Now I can go for dips in the pond as well. I am tired of buckets and bath-tubs and showers. My mother-in-law used to bathe here and once or twice she had taken me with her. It's a lovely feeling. But of course, the hyacinths had put an end to that."

Everyone was happy with the beginning Neel and Ratna had made, except Neel. There had been no gleam of gold in the dark depths of the pond. An expert swimmer, he had entered the pond again and again but there had been no buried pots or piles of gems.

"This will not do," Neel said to Ratna. We must make a thorough and systematic search of the entire area."

"We need some clues or hints, Neel-dada, at least to begin our search."

"True, we can't search at random."

They were standing by the side of the pond discussing all this. There was a mud road winding nearby. An old lady, quite bent and wrinkled, came up, carrying a basket of papayas on her snowy head. She had a hooked nose and a twisted smile.

For a second Ratna felt that she had seen her somewhere. But the feeling was gone in a flash.

"Kusum-dida (Granny), where are you off to?" Neel asked casually. She was most un-flower-like but well, Ratna realized, that was her name: Kusum or Flower.

"Going to the village market. See, these big papayas? From the tree in my courtyard. If I can sell them, I can get some money in my hand. I need it badly."

Kusum-dida had a small hut some distance away from the *kachhari* building. She had some land next to it where she had a papaya tree, a plantain grove, and bamboo lattices upon which grew pumpkins and gourds. She also grew coriander, chilli, and *saag*s like *pudina* and *kalmi*. When they were ready, she plucked and sold them at the village market.

Neel and Ratna began to walk with her, Neel began carrying the basket of papayas.

6

A Treatise on Money

"*Taka, taka i sawb* (Money, money is everything in the world)," Dida muttered, "Not just to me but to everybody. See, it is for money that the peasant toils in the field, the worker hammers away at the workshop, the shopkeeper spreads out his goodies. It is for money that people rack their brains, trick, and even kill others. All for the sake of money. It is for the money that I, the daughter of the Nayeb of Shalboni, do this."

Immediately Ratna realized why she had felt that she had seen her before. She had not. But she had seen the Nayeb with the crooked nose that her grand-daughter had inherited. However, she kept quiet. Who would believe her? She did not believe it fully herself!

Meanwhile, Kusum-dida kept rambling:

" All this for money! What is money, can you tell me? What does it actually do? Why did God create money?"

"Dida, it is not God who created money," answered Neel, "Money is entirely man-made. It is just a helpful invention by human beings."

"How so?" Old as she was, Kusum-dida seemed eager to learn. "There was a time", said Neel. "when there was no money in the world. Even then people used to work in the fields, they used to do a direct give and take between their products. They used to barter, say, crops for clothes, milk for fruits, oil for tools. But this ran into difficulties. Say, a peasant has reaped a rich harvest of crops. He wants an iron ploughshare. The village blacksmith does have an iron ploughshare. But he does not want grains, he wants clothes. The village weaver has clothes for him, but he does not want an iron ploughshare, he wants grains. The peasant has grains but just then he does not want new clothes."

He added, "There was another difficulty. Supposing the pleasant has got grains and does want a ploughshare. The blacksmith has got a ploughshare and does want grains. Even then they may not get to agree with each other. How much grain is to be given for a ploughshare? What is the worth of a ploughshare in terms of grain? How is grain to be compared with ploughshares? How is milk to be compared to clothes? See, only if grains, clothes, tools, and every other thing can be compared with another, can they be exchanged for one another? It is money which provides that common yardstick," said Neel.

"Get it, Dida?", asked Ratna, "The difficulties of barter made people turn slowly to the use of money. Not crops, not ploughshares, not clothes … but an additional something, a different something."

"Gold and silver and copper," Dida raised her eyes to the sky. They were shining through the film of cataract that covered them.

"Not necessarily so," said Neel. "It could be cowries from the seashore, dried berries, beads of glass or wood

… anything small and similar but found in big numbers. Let's take cowries or seashells. If the peasant is given cowries in place of his grains, then with those cowries he can get the ploughshare from the blacksmith who can use those cowries to get clothes from the weaver. The weaver too can use those cowries to get grains from the peasant. This changing of hands–for grains, tools, or clothes–was no longer direct but through money. That is why money is said to be a medium of exchange. It can do the job of being a medium because it is a common yardstick against which different things can be measured and compared. Suppose a kg of grains costs Rs 100 and a meter of cloth costs Rs 50. Then selling a kg of grains gives a peasant the power to buy 2 meters of cloth. It is thus that money makes exchange easier. It is nothing by itself."

The village market could be seen at a distance. There were many people walking or cycling along the road, most with items they wanted to sell in the market.

There was a shady Peepul tree by the roadside. Kusum-dida, Ratna, and Neel sat down below it. The sun was making the day hot.

Dida had a question. "What if the peasant or the blacksmith or the weaver –whoever it is – refuses to accept the cowries or beads or whatever it is?"

"That would be a problem," said Neel. "It is only because people accept it that money remains money. General acceptability is essential for anything to become money. The very word that is used for one kind of money – currency – shows this movement from hand to hand – like a current of flowing water ."

"But then as soon as people stop accepting a particular thing as money, it won't remain money anymore!" Dida frowned.

"Exactly," said Ratna, "Can we buy anything with cowries these days? For that matter, can we buy anything anymore with gold *mohur*s coined at the time of Badshah Akbar? Again, if we take Indian rupees to the United States, can we buy anything without first changing it to dollars?"

Dida clutched her head.

"It is now getting to be a bit too much for me. I should be getting to the market, anyway and get some money out of these papayas. But do come over to my place sometime tomorrow and tell me more. I do want to know."

Neel and Ratna helped her reach the market, where she spread a sack of jute and sat with her papayas.

Neel and Ratna moved away with the two papayas she gave them for free.

7

At the Railway Station

The village market was spread around a huge Banyan tree and mostly sold local products and produce. Villagers brought their home-grown fruits and vegetables, home-made pottery and artefacts. But there were some stalls that sold simple plastic or metal items, bangles and ribbons, spiced puffed rice, colourful iced drinks, and such other fancy items which were not available at the local provisions store.

They ran into Mita who was savouring a pink iced drink. Ratna had a sip and Neel said he was off all artificial drinks. Organic food and drinks were all he cared for.

"What's that, Neel-dada?" asked Mita. "Organic?"

But Ratna did not want Neel to launch another lecture just then. "Let's go to the railway station, shall we?" she said quickly as that was what had caught her eye from a distance.

They turned away from the market and sprinted towards the small railway station.

The fields stretched on either side – the land that had once made one person a landlord and the others his subjects. By now people were going about their day's work, taking goats out to graze, and cows to plough the fields. Once the fields ended, there lay the village 'commons' where everyone could graze their cattle. A train was coming into the station, pausing and moving away.

All around there was greenery. Trees and clumps of tall, waving grass. Panting, the three of them reached the station. Its raised platform was empty now. Red buckets of dirty sand hung outside the station master's room for protection against possible fire. The elderly station master sat in his room, looking utterly bored.

He was almost ready for a chat with Neel, Ratna, and Mita, especially when he learnt where they were from.

"Earlier this line had steam engines running on it. Bengal Express, Darjeeling Mail... But, of course, now it is only diesel trains that run."

Soon he was telling them about an accident of long ago.

"It happened at the time of Jomidar Ramesh-babu, your grandfather", he looked at Ratna. A kid of about eleven, a village lad named Shyamu, had been caught catching fish in the pond that lay within the Jomidar babu's grounds; the one that the rest of the village was not supposed to use. He had been caught by a guard, locked up all night, and then hauled up in the *kachhari* where Ramesh-babu used to sit.

"But he ran away from the *kachhari*, didn't he?" said Ratna.

"Yes, and made a dash for the railway station, but wait a bit, how come you know about this?"

Not just the station master but Neel and Mita too turned curious eyes upon Ratna.

"Oh, I just made a guess. Off-hand, you know. How would I know about it?"

"Can't keep quiet for a minute, is that it? Shall I stop, then?"

"No, Sir, no. Please go on. We'll be quiet."

The station master looked happy at being called `Sir' and went on.

"Well, Shyamu came rushing through the fields a guard came rushing after him. He caught hold of Shyamu and at that very second Shyamu took a wild leap towards the tracks. A steam engine, the Bengal Beauty, was hurtling towards the station. In an instant, the two of them were run down, and the train sped away with blood and gore upon its wheels."

"Terrible," all three said together.

"What is even more terrible is that on moonless nights the scene repeats itself."

"Have you seen it?" all three asked with awe.

"Well, no. But station-masters before me have."

"It is always `someone else' who has seen the ghost that the storyteller tells about," Neel commented softly. Mita smiled but Ratna did not.

On the way back, she was very quiet.

CHAPTER 3

8

An Old Recipe Book

At night Jethi-ma had made some exquisite sweets. Ma asked her for the recipe.

"It is a very old one. I found it in a *khata* (exercise book) that had belonged to Ramesh Chowdhuri's wife Soudamini Devi–our grandmother-in-law–Baro-ma (Bengali for Bari-ma). You know, she was not into cooking herself. She did not even enter the kitchen for fear of the smoke ruining her complexion. But she directed the cooks on the menu and measured out the *masala* herself from the larder. She collected recipes of all kinds, neatly written out by the Nayeb himself. "

"What! The Nayeb, writing down recipes for the Jomidar's wife!" Ma exclaimed.

"Baro-ma had a personality of her own. Her husband's employees were her employees. They obeyed her implicitly. Even the Nayeb."

"But where did you find Baro-ma's *khata*?"

"You won't believe when I tell you where I found it! In Kusum-dida's hut."

"What's the connection?" Payal's mother was astonished.

"She is the daughter of the old Nayeb of our grandfather-in-law Ramesh-babu,", Jethi-ma explained, "With the *jomidari* gone, the Nayeb's job was gone. His family sunk into poverty. The Nayeb himself passed away. His widowed daughter Kusum continued to live on in this village, all by herself. We treat her with respect and call her Kusum-didi or Kusum-dida."

"Well, how did you happen to find Baro-ma's copy there?"

"Once I had had to take shelter there because it had started to rain while I was out. My eyes had fallen upon a stack of old papers, ledgers, and registers that had the seal of our *jomidari*. The Nayeb must have kept them in his house, and so they stayed there, stacked in a corner with rats and cockroaches running across them. I fingered them and came upon this. Baro-ma's name `Soudamini Devi' was written upon it. The Nayeb must have made a mistake and taken this over to his place along with the rest and it had remained misplaced till I picked it up."

"Let's search for some more old recipes," said Ma.

Ratna went to sleep in a room upstairs, on an old wooden bed with elaborately carved bedposts. In the deep alcoves of the old mansion, bats flapped their wings.

9

Mita Gets A Fright

Early next morning, when the household was barely stirring, there was frantic banging upon the front door. As Neel opened it, Mita almost fell inside on the floor. "Somesh kaka! Neel-dada! Ratna! Come at once! I can't get Ma and Baba to wake up." The three of them rushed out with Mita to her house. Jetha too followed them. Mita's parents were still in bed but frothing at the mouths. A few other villagers were there. A woman from next doors was rubbing her mother's hands and feet. The pesticide container lay on its side on the floor: open, gaping, its cap open.

. "I got up this morning," said Mita, " and found it was already sunny. I wanted to hurry so that I would not be late for school. But then I wondered: why hadn't Ma woken me up? And why was the house so silent? I went to the kitchen and it was cold and fireless. Ma! Baba! I called and went to the next room. And I found, this!"

Neel picked the pesticide container, capped it, and took it to the courtyard. "Why, it doesn't even have the ISI mark. It is sub-standard stuff."

Ratna knew that ISI mark stands for the stamp of the Indian Standards Institute, set up when India gained Independence to create standards to which products should conform. Later a stronger body, the Bureau of Indian Standards (BIS), took over ISI. But "ISI mark" is still the term used.

"Last evening, I heard Baba and Ma talk of the hard times they were having. Their tones got sadder and sadder as they went on. The new pesticide had not worked at all. For the paddy crops were once again infected with `Walker'."

"That's Tryporyza incertulas," said Neel-dada but nobody heard him as Mita continued with her story.

"Soon Ma began to cry. But I was feeling so tired myself so I went to sleep. I did not even imagine that they would try to take their own lives."

"In Odissa and Andhra also farmers have committed suicide," one of the neighbours lamented.

"Still, for our Bhupen to have done it!"

"Not a thought for the child!"

"Stop all this," Jetha spoke firmly and loudly.

"Neel, get the car here". Baba used his mobile to call the local hospital and instructed them that they were rushing two poison-victims there. Neel had driven the car from the mansion and brought as close as possible as the lane leading to this house was narrow. Mita's parents were carried to the back seat. Ratna and Mita got in, holding the two unconscious ones who kept slipping down.

Neel drove the car along the uneven rural road, Ratna's father by his side. Jetha walked home, discussing the matter with others.

The other villagers followed, some on their cycles, some on foot. The hospital was beyond the railway station. Fortunately, no train was passing just then, and so, time was not wasted at the level-crossing.

The young doctor at the hospital, as Ratna saw, made Baba call the police first but did not make any delay in attending to his patient. Two attendants wheeled Mita's parents to the Emergency Room. Everybody stood outside, anxiously waiting for the doctor.

After an hour or so, the doctor came out of the Emergency Room and declared that the patients were out of danger. Of course, they had to stay on in the hospital for a couple of days. Local policemen arrived since it was a matter of attempted suicide. Ratna's father and some village seniors talked to them and sent them away.

While her parents were away at the hospital, neighbours close by took care of Mita. Kusum-dida asked Mita to move in with her till her parents were back.

So the next day, once everyone had made a round of the hospital, Ratna went over to dida's house to spend some time with Mita.

10

At Kusum-dida's Hut

Dida was arguing with Moti, a village lad.

A scrawny lad with hollows around his small eyes. He had big white teeth bared in a lopsided smile. Ratna knew by now that he was a helper in the village provision store. It was the *mahajan* or moneylender, Vishnu Poddar, who owned the provision store. His father Jishnu Poddar had set it up.

"Go tell Vishnu that I don't have the money to pay for the mustard oil I bought last Monday. He knows perfectly well that I don't."

"Dida, didn't you make some money this week at the market? I saw you!"

"Well, that's all gone, Moti. Off you go, take this papaya for yourself. Tell Vishnu he must wait."

Moti grinned and went away with his papaya.

Dida offered some to her guest.

What a juicy one it was!

"I could come here only for these papayas", thought Ratna. "But I must find out if she still has those stacks of *jomidari* papers."

Sure enough, she did.

"Why have you kept them all this time, Dida? They take up space and are so full of dust. Eeeks! That's a cockroach!"

"Throw them away," suggested Mita, "Burn them up."

"Don't you say that again," Dida said angrily. "They are all I have. No money, nothing. All I have of my great-grandfather the Nayeb are those papers. They mean more than money to me."

Ratna put a hand round her. "Yes, they are indeed valuable pieces of the past. Can we just look through them – they look so quaint!"

Most were just wads of long rough paper, off-white with age, sewn together under a long red cloth cover and folded back. Some were legal documents in stamp paper of the British era. A few were diaries with velvet covers and metal clasps. The clasps had rusted and gave way only when one put force on them. The writings were in neat small Bengali letters. Inside, on the front page, in golden lettering that still gleamed, there was the name `Ramesh Chowdhuri'.

Why they could contain clues to where the treasure was. Ratna begged permission to take them home to read at leisure.

"I want them back, Ratna Didi," answered the old woman, "Remember, I am just lending them to you. Your aunt borrowed a diary and never gave it back!"

Ah, the recipe book that the Nayeb had copied out for the Jomidar's wife.

Mita promised to check if there was anything more of interest in the stack. Her *charpoy* had been placed in that room.

Her parents were recovering but it would be a couple of more days before they were back.

11

The Diaries

Back at home, Ratna compared the handwriting of the diary with the one in Jethi-ma's recipe book. This was a different, rather untidy–Ramesh-babu's own. No wonder Soudamini Devi preferred the Nayeb as her scribe rather than her husband.

She showed this to Neel, and together they began to go through them.

One was written in the year 1918.

"A strange news has come. In Russia, the Emperor has been captured and killed by the common people. The people have taken over the control of the country and declared that land will no longer be private property. No one will be able to own land. It will belong to the State but there will be no emperor or king to head the State. All citizens will have equal rights over the land. They will all own it in a joint or united way. Farming will be done through State-run Collective Farms. Cannot make head or tail of all this."

Before she knew it, Neel-dada had launched forth into a lecture.

"The Soviet Union, formed after a violent October Revolution of 1917, had inherited an economy which, although it had some industrial units, was basically agricultural and feudal. Their leader, Lenin, had wanted *smychka*–an alliance between peasants and workers. But when in 1929 the Soviet Union decided to have five-year plans. While doing this they discovered that savings were required from peasants to serve the needs of workers. The agricultural surplus was needed for the industrial sector. Joseph Stalin who was the leader then managed to achieve this in an unexpected and extreme way–Collectivization of agriculture.

Peasant landholdings and livestock were forcibly brought together into collective farms (*kolkhozy*). These farms had to deliver certain planned amounts to the State at terms dictated by the state. *Sovkhozy* or State farms were also formed. K*olkhozy* were peasants' farms re-organized while *sovkhozy* were farms newly set up under the State.

Now, the rich peasants or *kulaks* had not developed the new attitude or mindset that was required for Socialism to work. They were not ready for a collectivization or nationalization of land and livestock as means of production. Violence had to be used upon them. There was bloodshed.

"Reports of this must have come to India", said Neel as he ended his lecture, "and this is what Jomidar Ramesh Chowdhuri wrote in his diary.

Neel turned the pages and chuckled.

"I am thinking of naming my newborn son Suresh. Have asked Nayeb-moshai to make all the arrangements."

Ratna giggled.

"Neel! Ratna! Come! Food is ready!"

12

Mita's Fears

Next day Mita brought some good news. Her parents were well enough to be released from the hospital. Ratna's father, Dwijesh Chowdhuri asked Neel to take the car out once again to the hospital.

"Bhupen is an old friend", he said. "Besides, what is our car there for, if not for use of the people around us?"

Together Neel and Ratna dropped Mita's parents at their home. Ratna hung around Mita, tidying up. It had become dusty while Mita was away at Dida's. Besides, her parents still needed bed-rest and a patient's diet. Neighbours gathered around. Some wanted to help. Some were plain curious.

"Why did you take the pesticide?"

"I did not have money to pay Vishnu *mahajan*," said Bhupen-kaka. "I tried to raise the money. I even sold the few ornaments she had," Bhupen-kaka pointed to Mita's mother who was leaning weakly against a pillow, "Whatever we did, it was not enough. He threatened to bring a case against me – or take the land away."

"How could he do that?" one of the neighbours asked, "unless you had signed something silly?"

Bhupen-kaka hung his head.

"Why didn't you ask us for aid?" asked another, "Not that we could have given you much being needy ourselves".

"I did ask you once if you remember, and you refused."

"Well, well," said the man. "We are all in the same boat here. But why didn't you ask Dwijesh-babu for a loan? They were once the *jomidar*s here."

"Or Somesh-babu who has just come? Didn't you go to *pathshala* together?"

"He visited you.. we saw!" another chipped in.

"He is your friend."

"That is exactly why I did not want to touch him for a loan," Bhupen-kaka replied.v

His wife pointed at Ratna and made a silent plea not to discuss this further in front of her. Ratna saw it. She sensed that a certain distance still existed between the villagers and the family of the erstwhile landlords.

Once her parents were back, daily life came slowly back to the what it used to be. Ma was soon able to cook and clean, and Mita began to help her by doing simple chores on her way to and from school.

Her father could not go back to the fields just then and took-up basket-weaving for the time being.

This was something his wife and daughter could help in. Kusum-dida did her bit by taking them to the local market to sell.

The backyard slowly piled up with baskets. The pesticide container, tightly capped, was moved to one side.

Yes, life came back to the old pattern, except for the dark rings around Mita's eyes.

She confided in Ratna that her sleeping pattern was all messed up. She would get up every now and then in her sleep, in a panic that her parents had again consumed pesticide. She would tip-toe into their room, peer into their faces, and say to herself, "No, their breathing is alright and there is no foam on their lips". Then she would come back to her room and fall asleep, only to jerk awake in an hour or so. "What if that container of pesticides is still there in that room? Within their easy reach? I must take it away." Of course, the container was no longer there, but Mita was haunted by it.

CHAPTER 4

13

Julian and Tessa

Meanwhile, other things had happened. Two of Neel's friends from abroad had arrived. Neel had travelled up to the Kolkata airport and brought them down to Shalboni.

Julian and Tessa were staying at the mansion with Ratna and the rest.

Julian was thin and tall and bearded. He wore bead necklaces, torn clothes, and sang folk songs of Bengal. Tessa too was thin and tall and wore a nose ring. The brother and sister duo were both "into Organic stuff" which is why on their trip to India, they had come to visit Neel's organic farm.

"How did they become your friends, Neel-dada?"

"My college in Kolkata has an exchange program with an American University. Foreign students come to India and Indian students go abroad for short terms. That's how I had gone to the U.S.A. and met Julian and Tessa who taught a course at the university there."

Neel and Ratna, Julian and Tessa, walked across the village. The villagers stopped and turned to look. Julian and Tessa called out cheery little `Hi's to them. Some of them stared. Some of them brought their hands together in a *namaskar*.

There were no fences between the fragments or pieces of fields, but borders made of raised mounds of earth.

"Much arable land goes waste in India due to this manner of marking boundaries. They are all part of rich, fertile land but are not cultivated," Neel pointed out to Julian and Tessa.

"Ah, there's your signboard," Julian exclaimed.

Planted solidly upon the ground was a board saying Organic in Hindi, and the picture of a pesticide can with a cross in thick black lines drawn over it.

"I put it up so that those working on the nearby fields do not turn their sprays on mine. You see, organic farming is a new concept. Chemical fertilizers and sprays are what these farmers use. But when you spread chemicals upon your own field, you can't help some of it getting into your neighbour's field whether he wants it or not."

When they actually entered Neel's fields, they were ecstatic.

"Not a drop of chemical fertilizer has been used," Neel announced, "Not a drop of pesticide has been sprayed upon them."

"But aren't chemical fertilizers and pesticides good for the fields?" Ratna could not help asking.

“That is what people thought once upon a time in the mid-1960s,” replied Neel. “After independence, in 1947, various reforms were made to agricultural landholding patterns. These were institutional reforms, changing land tenure systems established in Mughal and British times. Abolition of Intermediaries Act and Land Ceiling Act of the 1950s are the prime examples. But food shortage became so acute in the 1960s that technological – not just institutional – changes were considered essential. That is when High Yielding Varieties (HYV), chemical fertilizers, and pesticides were developed by scientists in India and encouraged by the government. With improved irrigation, the government was so successful in raising crop yield in Punjab, Haryana, and Uttar Pradesh that it seemed like a revolution – the Green Revolution. ”

“Yes”, Ratna chipped in, “ I have often passed the Pusa Institute in Delhi and seen the Pusa Harit Kranti Park at Rajinder Nagar.”

“But ——”, began Neel.

14

Green Revolution and Organic Farming

"But initially, the Green Revolution happened only in the north and among farmers who could afford the new technology. So, it led to disparities among regions as well as people. Then again, boring too many tube wells for irrigation lowered the groundwater table. Chemical pesticides and fertilizers harmed soil fertility as well as human digestion."

Many people began to lose their enthusiasm for the Green Revolution, with its expensive yet harmful fertilizers and pesticides."

"Not just in India but in the world", put in Julian.

"Do pesticides mean a lot of costs as well for the farmer?" asked Ratna.

"Of course! Whenever he has to buy it for himself, he finds himself paying a lot of money, sometimes to big companies, even multinationals. He borrows the money, hoping for results that will recover his costs. But what if the results are not good enough?"

Neel paused and looked at Julian and Tessa.

"If the harvest is bad, say, for two years running, a farmer may not be able to repay the loan he had taken to pay for his expensive technology. He may be forced to sell the land – sometimes to foreign-owned farming operations. He may become a landless labourer and move to a city. He may even be driven to commit suicide. Thousands have actually done so.

"In fact, a week ago there was such an incident in our own village," Neel told Julian and Tessa about Mita's parents consuming the very pesticide they had purchased.

Initially, the government had provided seeds, fertilizers, and pesticides for free to the farmers in order to give them the incentive to use them. But once that the idea has caught on, private companies have begun to make and sell pesticides and fertilizers. Even multinational companies have stepped in. Not all these products are suitable to the Indian soil. Sometimes they are toxic. They kill the pests but also kill the natural fertility of the soil.

And kill the farmer when he consumes it himself!

"That's it", said Tessa forcefully. "Expensive. Poisonous. Prone to misuse. Better do away with them altogether."

"But Tessa," Ratna chipped in, "How do we then deal with the pests that trouble the crops?"

"I am sure there are ways – Indian ways–traditional ways- which everyone has forgotten," answered Tessa. "Neem-based bio-pesticides are already being developed."

"Our NGO wants to research such techniques. If there is a promising project to develop environment-sensitive yet effective biopesticides, we can fund it," offered Julian.

Julian and Tessa belonged to a small organization based in the U.S. that spread the message of Organic Farming to developing countries like India. They believe that the world today uses an excess of synthetic and artificial products and equipment.

Neel-dada was their enthusiastic supporter.

The fresh air blew sweetly over the paddy fields untouched by anything artificial. A small river could be seen in the distance. The railway tracks ran across the bridge over the river.

The fields were so green that Ratna felt like lying down and going to sleep.

But the walk and the fresh air had made them hungry. In one of the fields, Neel had planted carrots instead of paddy. He uprooted a few and offered them to the others. They bit into them, raw and unwashed.

“Can’t be more toxic than pesticides,” joked Tessa. Her nose-ring flashed in the golden sunlight.

15
The Riverside

Then they walked up to the river. Tessa stumbled once upon the uneven ground. Ratna caught her and prevented a sprain. Neel and Julian walked ahead of them. A goods train could be seen coming out of the station and moving across the bridge. By the time they reached the bridge, it had passed. The bridge was not a big one and had gaps between the ancient wooden bars that held the rails in place. Even the nuts and bolts fastening the bars were `Made in England'. While the British had brought railways to India and transformed her transport sector forever, they had largely used their own products. This was true not only for the engines, the carriages, and the tracks but for the nuts and bolts as well. By getting them made in England, the British encouraged the growth of iron and steel industry in their home country. Indian iron and steel industry did not get much boost from the railways being built in India.

Balancing on those ancient bars, they could see the river through their gaps. Women were washing clothes in the river and flinging them out on some rocks jutting out of the waters. Two buffaloes were being bathed by a boy who clearly was in charge of them. A yellow sign-board gave the name of the river in black railway lettering: Jaltungi.

A white crane flew down upon a buffalo's back.

"See it pecking at the worms on the buffalo?" said Neel. "That's ecological balance for you."

"Yes, the worms, the crane, the buffalo and the boy –are all bound together. Once this place grows, that balance will be disturbed," agreed Tessa.

"But then that boy will perhaps be able to go to school", said Ratna, "instead of tending buffaloes".

Somehow the sight of that boy reminded her of Shyamu who had lost his life years ago. Merely on account of trespassing upon in a landlord's pond.

How much had life changed in the villages around here?

Didn't they need technology and modernity and a new way of life?

16

Reading Together

That night Neel and Ratna showed Julian and Tessa the diaries they had found at Kusum-dida's house.

Although they could not read Bengali, they could see how old it was and how it held valuable records of events and opinions.

In the diary of 1919, Jomidar Ramesh Chowdhuri wrote: " The Government Of India Act 1919–that is, the Montford Reform – has been passed and it has made irrigation a provincial subject. Henceforth, the British will not bother much with it. Cultivation will suffer neglect."

Elsewhere, he wrote: "I was fortunate enough to visit Amritsar in my early years. At Jalliwanwalla Bagh, two days earlier, that is, on April 13, one General Dyer opened fire upon people in a peaceful protest meeting. What is more, Michael O'Dwyer, the Governor of Punjab, defended the action. Sir Rabindranath Tagore, I hear, has returned his knighthood in protest. He will no longer be `Sir Rabindranath Tagore'. But what does that great poet care? His grandfather Dwarakanath Tagore was, of course, a different kind of person. I have heard that he was a very efficient and exacting landlord as well as a pioneer in commerce and industry, who mixed a lot with the British gentry."

In the 1920 diary, Ramesh Chowdhuri had referred to the plentiful rains and good harvests. In 1921, he noted that the Prince of Wales had visited India but was greeted by a bonfire of foreign clothes – as a symbolic destruction of British Indian products inspired by Africa-returned barrister M. K. Gandhi.

In 1922 he wondered at Gandhi's calling off the Civil Disobedience Movement. In 1926 he mentioned the Royal Commission on Agriculture. No major changes occurred in respect of land ownership. That seemed a relief to him.

The late 1920s found him preoccupied with the Collectivization operations in the Soviet Union.

"That Stalin!" he wrote, "Taking away the property of the landed gentry and even killing them off. What if such ideas caught on here?"

On 26 January 1930 he wrote: "At the stroke of midnight on December 31, 1929, at Lahore, M.K.Gandhi has led the Indian National Congress to vow that nothing less than `Purna Swaraj' will do for India. 26 January 1930 is being called the Purna Swaraj Divas. Now the question is, what is going to happen to the *jomidari* once Purna Swaraj is here? Are we all going to be killed like the *kulak*s in Russia?"

Julian and Neel began to laugh.

The Dandi March of 1930, the shifting of government offices from Old Delhi to the New Delhi, the establishment of the Reserve Bank of India, and Government of India Act 1935 were mentioned. But Ramesh Chowdhuri –middle-aged by now–did not seem to react much to them. He was more concerned with what would happen to his *jomidari* once Independence was achieved.

"Look," Ratna pointed to some later lines.

"Have taken a decision and asked Nayeb-moshai to go ahead with the tunnel. Only Haru *lathiyal* is to know."

"What is this tunnel?" Julian asked.

"Oh, there is supposed to be some ancestral treasure lying about underground", Neel said with a laugh. "Maybe the tunnel leads to it!"

"Ancestral treasure?" Julian and Tessa perked up at once.

Now that Neel had carelessly mentioned it, he had to explain.

"Not treasure, maybe. But certainly, family valuables. Gold, silver, and jewellery. Well, I have heard of it in my childhood. My parents saying how wonderful it would be if we could find it. But it has never been found."

Neel's voice trailed off.

"That is because it has never been looked for", said Ratna at once. "I am sure we can find it if we look for it. Now that we know there really is a tunnel, I am sure there is treasure at the end of it."

"Oh, I wish we could stay here for a few more days and join the treasure hunt," exclaimed Tessa. "But we are off to Amodpur tomorrow."

"Amodpur…isn't it further along the rail-line we saw this morning?" asked Ratna.

"Yes, that's one reason why we stopped here, apart from looking up this guy here, of course", Julian slapped Neel's back.

"But why are you going to Amodpur of all places?"

"To meet the Bauls of Amodpur", said Tessa. "I love Baul songs."

Julian began to hum one.

"*Amar jemon beni temni robe....*"

Ratna was surprised. Bauls were the roaming minstrels of the Birbhum district of Bengal, strumming on a single-stringed musical instrument called *ektara*.

"How come you can sing Baul songs, Julian?"

"Well, in New York we have this centre for folk songs. That is where I met a Baul from India who had gone there for a performance. I was bowled over. What music, what philosophy!"

"Amar jemon beni temni robe

Chul bhijabo na.

Jale nabbo jal chhitabo

Jal to chhonbo na".

My plait shall remain as it is, my hair I will not wet.

I will enter the waters and sprinkle it around

My hand wet, I will not get.

"This is indeed the philosophy of the Bauls", said Neel, "Live your life but do not get involved in it. Share everything but do not get stuck. Well, don't forget to message me once you are at Amodpur."

"We intend to video-chat," said Julian.

The conversation turned to the Bauls. Ratna put away the diaries.

CHAPTER 5

17

Blood on the Snow

The next day Julian and Tessa took the train to Amodpur, accompanied by Neel.

After doing her homework for school, Ratna went across to Mita.

She found her tending to the cooking.

"I am still weak," said her mother from the bed. "So Mita does most of the chores.

Her father looked up from the baskets he was making.

"I can't bear to see her do it and cannot sleep at night for worry. How shall I repay the *mahajan* or, for that matter, feed my family?"

"I know", groaned his wife. "I feel like -".

"Think positive, Bhupen-kaka," Ratna was ready to mouth. But before she could, Mita ran out of the kitchen and clutched her father.

"No Baba, don't swallow it again."

"Swallow what?" Her mother said, surprised, but her father understood and hugged her tightly.

"Don't die on me," sobbed Mita, "Don't swallow that pesticide again."

" *Na re na*", cried her mother." It was a moment of madness in which we even forgot you."

"What is more," said Bhupen-kaka, "I am thinking of not using pesticides on my fields even when I am strong enough to get back to them. Neel has been talking to me, and I see the sense in what he is saying."

"Mita, go out and spend some time with Ratna," said her mother, "You should not be cooped up with us all day."

The two of them went to visit Kusum-dida.

"Dida!" Mita called.

"Silly! Don't you see the latch?" said Ratna.

The door had its latch pulled up from the outside. Dida must have gone out to the village market to sell some of her home-grown fruits and vegetables. But then the basket in which she usually carried her stuff was there, leaning on the earthen wall. What did it mean?

The two of them hovered outside and suddenly heard a muffled groan coming from within the house. Unlatching the door, they were inside in an instant.

The old lady was lying on the floor. She was groaning but unconscious.

"Now it is she who has swallowed the pesticide!" screamed Mita, almost fainting.

“Silly!” said Ratna once again. “Don’t you see she has been hit on the head?”

There was blood on the snowy hair…

Mita rushed out to call the neighbours. Ratna sprinkled water on Dida’s face.

Dida’s chest was rising and falling but her eyes remained closed.

There was something else she observed with a sense of shock. The stack of old legal documents was gone! Only a few torn scraps lay there in that corner, among the droppings of the mice and lizards that had thrived there all this while.

18

Down in the Depths

The villagers crowded in and Ratna saw her father arrive. She felt a surge of relief. Bhupen-kaka too, weak as he was, walked in. The local police were called and Ratna's father himself drove Dida to the hospital in his car.

Mita took her father home. She did not want him to get overstrained. Ratna walked back aimlessly until she found herself before the old *kachhari* house again.

The long wooden shutters were unwelcoming but Ratna felt that she must get in.

The long shadowy room, floored in marble....

The Venetian-glass chandeliers...

The Jomidar-babu's couch....

"No one has sat on it for years," she thought. "Let me see how it feels to sit on it."

Step by step, Ratna approached it and sat down

It was dusty but really soft.

There was a foot-rest as well. She reclined on the couch and reached for the foot-rest. As her feet did not quite reach it, she tried to pull it closer. It refused to move and, irritated, she gave it a kick.

Ratna did not even have the time to scream. A trap door opened under her and she descended into the dark.

19

Groping About

It was not a long descent though and did not hurt Ratna as she had fallen on big bunches of paper that made a bed of sorts for her.

She had fallen into a small secret chamber full of old official documents and cardboard files.

There was a musty smell and Ratna began to feel suffocated.

She tried to get out but the trap door above had got shut by itself. Ratna tried to open it. But all that happened was that her fingers began to hurt. She tried to call for help. But all that happened was that her voice began to crack.

"Surely Ma and Baba are going to miss me, Jethi-ma, and the others? Surely they will come to my rescue?" thought Ratna, "But then nobody saw me going to the *kachhari*. Nobody would think I would be going into it. Even if they did come here by chance, nobody knows that there is a trapdoor here and a secret chamber underneath. Nobody will find me and I will just lie here starving to death."

It was not a cheerful idea.

"Think positive", Ratna told herself, "At least, think!"

Going to each corner of the chamber, she tried to find out if there was a loose brick or some other opening. Sure enough, there was a brick that moved under her touch. As soon as Ratna ferreted it out, she found another one giving away. And another.

Soon there was a small opening revealing a set of stairs slanting going downward.

The air was getting musty. Ratna felt like fainting. But she squeezed through the opening and groped down the stairs.

"There must be an end to it," she kept telling herself, "This must be the tunnel that the diary mentioned and it must have had a purpose."

The stairs broadened and split into two. Which way to take?

Ratna felt her head go round and round. But she reasoned that she should take the one that smelt mustier.

"It must be leading to water, and that means some opening."

On the wall, there were shiny streaks. Silver? Melted and put in the cracks? No, they were just lines left by moving snails.

The walls were wet and mossy by now, and Ratna could smell the damp, stinky air. Ah, there was mud, and grass, and sunshine on them! Ratna had emerged onto the bank of the pond…right through the dump of hyacinths it had been cleared off.

While clearing the pond, they had happened to fling the hyacinths right on the tunnel exit, and so had missed it completely!

Ratna shook off some hyacinths from her hair. How comforting the dump looked! What a pretty colour mauve was!

Jethi-ma and Ma were surprised to see Ratna return so muddy and untidy. "Where were you?" "Did you have a fall or something?" they kept asking.

Ratna wanted to blurt out her underground adventure but she was afraid of being scolded. "Why did you go to the *kachhari* all by yourself?" Ma was likely to say. "Never are you to go there again", Jethi-ma might order.

So Ratna kept quiet. In any case, Ma and Jethi-ma were taken up by Kusum-dida's news.

"Who could have done it?"

They kept on asking themselves as well as Ratna.

Neel arrived late in the evening. Julian and Tessa had stayed on at Amodpur. Almost instantly he took the car out to the hospital to get updates on Kusum-dida.

"Our Neel is such a caring person," said Ma.

"He is, " said Jethi-ma, " Besides, our family has a responsibility towards the old lady. Poor as she is now, she is the grand-daughter of the Nayeb of Jomidar Ramesh Chowdhuri. Even Ramesh Chowdhuri used to address him with respect as Nayeb-moshai."

Ratna's fingers, toes, and her whole body was hurting. She went away to her room and fell asleep quickly.

20

Silently and Secretly

The next morning Neel told them that he had called the hospital and that Kusum-dida had slipped into a coma. Unless she came out of it, there would be no new information on who had attacked her and why.

Could it be Moti, wondered Ratna? Hadn't he come that day to badger Dida for money? But then what would he gain by hitting her so brutally? But first, she must tell Neel-dada about her own adventure.

Neel was stunned and overjoyed when Ratna told him about the secret passages she had yesterday tumbled into.

" I see", Neel clutched at his hair. "The mouth of the passage opened towards the pond and we had thrown the hyacinths to that side. Fools! Blocking up the very thing we were after! ..... But you said that the passage splits. Where does the other part of the passage lead to?"

"We must find that out, Neel-dada!"

"Yes, we will go tonight."

"Go to sleep early. I will come and call you around midnight, and we shall go."

"Neel-dada, shall we tell Mita ?"

"Not now. In any case, she has to be with her parents in the night."

Jethi-ma had made delicious fried rice for dinner but Ratna dared not stuff herself up with it. Instead, she took an extra *sandesh* or two and filled up a flask with water. They might need it if the passage was too long. Around midnight, Neel came to Ratna. He carried his cell phone with its inbuilt torch as well as a long steel ruler.

There was no need to open the main door. The mansion had huge windows with old-fashioned rods inserted in wooden frames instead of modern grilles in fancy designs. One or two of the windows had gaps where the rods had fallen off. Neel guided Ratna to one such window and together they got out of the house.

The moonlight reflected on the clear surface of the pond now that it had been cleared of hyacinth. Only a few of the nearby houses had lights on. Anyway, they were dim and mostly shaded by foliage.

There! They had reached the opening. Neel stepped into it, pulling Ratna with his left hand while holding the torch with his right. Once inside the tunnel, he switched the torch on.

Going ahead, they came to the spot where the tunnel from the *kachhari* end had come down and had broken into two.

"If we continue going this way, we'll reach the *kachhari*", whispered Ratna, "That's the way I came." In the dank underground tunnel, her voice seemed to boom.

"We'll go the other way," Neel's voice boomed back.

The two walked on. There was a sudden movement – a snake slithered away. Ratna froze. "It is a non-poisonous one," Neel pulled her closer to himself.

The other path had gone on a slight downwards incline and opened on to the pond. Ratna noticed that this one was inclined upwards. Very slowly, they were going up.

Then they suddenly came upon a small flat stretch of the floor full of – no, it can't be true!

Pesticide containers, green plastic ones just as Mita's parents had got.

After all this, pesticides!

They plonked down on the floor. Both needed a drink of water. Ratna brought out two of the *sandesh* pieces she was carrying. Looking around they saw footprints on the dust. They must belong to the men who had stacked pesticides here.

Neel-dada showed the cell phone torch upon the pesticide containers. "Do you see something? All of them do not have the ISI mark. Like the one Bhupen-kaka had bought."

From a crack in the ceiling, there came a ray of sunshine. It was morning!

Quickly they got up and went past the pesticides to some stairs at the other end. While it was part of the tunnel, it was no longer flat. Rough-hewn steps were clearing and taking them upwards.

The tunnel ended in a door which had clearly never been opened from this side. It was only latched, not locked, but the grime and grease of decades had jammed it. It took Neel ages to be able to unlatch the door.

Although it was still quite dark in the passage, Ratna closed her eyes and imagined that they would open into a gold-lined room. Walls of gold bricks, flooring of gold tiles, and chests heaped with precious jewels.

Ratna opened her eyes and stepped out.

Neel had to hold her as she took that step – and stepped into her own room.

The very one they had left at 4 am.

What a let-down.

21

Prasad Karmakar and his Artefacts

Neel left with a pat on Ratna's drooping head. "We'll talk about it later," he whispered.

"Time to get up, Ratna", Ma called from downstairs. Ratna quickly washed, changed her clothes, and went down.

She found her Jetha Dwijesh Chowdhuri sitting at the head of the marble-topped-table, the one at which they had their lunch, dinner and breakfast. Jetha sat at its head and looked rather grim.

"Som, that fellow will be here today. That hotelier with his wife who wants to start a resort here."

"All right, Dada(elder brother)", said Ratna's father Somesh Chowdhuri. "We will show him the papers so that he can `search' and check out the *daag* (Plot Number in the Field Index register at the district records office)."

"That means we are agreed on this? The property is indeed to be sold to him?"

A shining blue Audi whizzed in before the mansion. Two people got out and looked at the mansion. One of them was a young man in a smartly cut suit. The other was a young lady in *salwar kameez* of ethnic print. They looked familiar and Ratna realized why. They looked like they belonged to Delhi or the NCR (National Capital Region) rather than Kolkata or West Bengal. They certainly were not locals.

Jetha and Baba left their breakfast and hurried out to welcome them into the living room.

"*Aiye, aiye* ... "

Jethi-ma and Ma cleared the table quickly so that the guests could perhaps be served there later.

Ratna went to take a peek into Neel's room and found him fast asleep. No wonder he had not come down for breakfast.

For the last two days, Ratna had not met Mita. She went over to her place now. As soon as she reached, Bhupen-kaka asked her about the visitors. Everyone in the village had seen the blue Audi arrive and were curious.

"Oh, just some people to see Baba," Ratna countered the curious query. She pressed instead for news of Kusum-dida.

Still, in a coma, she learnt.

"Let's go and dust her place up," said Mita, " so that it is not too bad when she comes back."

But Bhupen-kaka was not done with his inquiries. "You know, we have seen that car earlier as well in the village. Parked a little ahead because it could go further down this narrow lane. Two people – a couple – had got down and gone towards Kusum-didi's house."

That surprised both Ratna and Mita. What did these people want with Kusum-dida?

Ratna and Mita started out. A village stray began to follow them. It was a brown mongrel but so well-behaved that Ratna did not mind it at her heels.

"Bhulo used to hang around Kusum-dida's house," Mita said, "He must be missing her."

Before they could reach the house, Binu came cycling along the narrow lane, stumbled and crashed against Ratna.

He folded his palms abjectly and said, "Didn't mean to do that. Ratna-didi, are you hurt?"

Although Binu was a couple of years older than Ratna, he called Ratna `*didi*'. It was a rural courtesy.

"Of course not. But Binu, where have you been all this while? We did not see you after we cleared the pond," said Ratna.

"Where are you going?" asked Mita.

"I have been apprenticed to Prasad Karmakar and that's where I am going now."

He got up on his cycle and was gone.

"Wait!" Neel-dada was coming along the same lane. "I got up and found those characters at home. So I decided to get out."

When asked, Neel explained to Ratna about Prasad Karmakar.

As the title Karmakar indicated, he was a blacksmith. His family went back to the days when the village had its own potter, weaver, and blacksmith, and the railway line too had not been built. Those were the days of `self-sufficient village economy'. With railways bringing in tools and equipment from outside, the blacksmiths lost much of their clients within the village. As they did not have land of their own, they began to work in the fields of others for money. They became labourers, only agricultural ones rather than industrial.

Ratna was scared that Neel would launch into an account of how the self-sufficient village economy died away. But Neel had more interesting things to say about Prasad Karmakar:

"Unlike many other blacksmiths, the Karmakars had not given up his family trade and become agricultural labourers. They had branched into making exquisite Dokra (Dhokra)crafts."

"I have seen Dokra crafts," said Ratna. "We have a Dokra elephant placed in our sitting room in Delhi. Ma got it from Dilli Haat and everybody admires it. She has also got a bead necklace with a Dokra owl as a pendant. But what Dokra is – I do not know."

"What *is* Dokra, Neel-dada?" asked Mita. "I too do not know exactly, although I do belong here."

"It is a very ancient way of metal-casting, using clay, wax, resin, and molten brass. They knew it at Mohen-jo-daro!" Neel joked.

"But Prasad is more than a Dokra-Kamar, that is, a tribal blacksmith doing Dokra. He claims that he adds a special ingredient which makes it unbreakable. Now the more durable an artefact is, the easier it is to pack and sell it in distant markets. So, Prasad Karmakar's Dokra-ware has high demand, especially as he does not tell anybody what the special ingredient is that gives his product its extra durability. But why has Binu become his apprentice? I wonder."

He pondered for a while and said:

"Now I remember Baba saying that Binu's father – who is his friend–had developed a dry cough that is simply not going away. Maybe Binu needs to work."

22

The Dokra Workshop

Kusum-dida's garden was full of papayas and jamuns. Ratna did not feel like looking at them, with Dida still lying in a coma at the hospital.

Mita took a broom to sweep the earthen floor. Where the papers had been stacked, Ratna saw a sort of shallow hole reveal itself. A few scraps of paper still lay there among the droppings of rats. Could this possibly be another trap door? Or an entry to another tunnel?

"Get back, get back!" called Mita. For, something had begun to peep out of the hole. A huge rat with its entire family behind him.

Even Neel-dada said, "Let's get out of here."

Latching the house from outside, the three of them went towards Mita's house.

"Ma, do we have a rat-trap around?" she asked.

But when she explained why it was required, her mother was doubtful about their going there again.

"Mita, there's no need for your kids to go there. Let Kusum-didi recover. There will be people to clean her house and take care of her. And you," she turned to Ratna, "don't worry so much about these village matters. You have just come here for your holidays."

"But", Neel began to say something. But Mita's mother stopped him. "Go home and see if your mothers say any different!"

Going home they found the Audi gone. But Jetha and Baba were sitting with glum faces. Jethi-Ma was not looking cheerful either.

"One day they will be living here – I feel terrible when I think of it."

"Come on, Didi, accept the inevitable", Ma comforted her.

But Jethi-Ma did not get comforted.

She turned to Baba and said, "Somesh-Thakur-po, are we doing the right thing?"

Ratna wondered if she should confide in Ma, but there was such a lot to confide! Instead, she talked about the Dokra workshop in the village and found Ma was interested in visiting it.

"I want to see how Dokra is done! And pick some pieces from the workshop. My friends in Delhi will love them."

Neel drove them out through the village. The old car looked shabby. But Neel drove it pretty smoothly over the uneven rural roads. Ah, there stood the workshop with its tin roof. Binu saw them and ran to fetch Prasad Karmakar, a dark, well-built man with muscular arms.

"It's an honour to have you here," he said. "Once the Karmakars used to work for the Jomidar-babus themselves. They got regular orders for making sickles and ploughshares. Even when my forefathers turned to Dokra, they had the last jomidar Ramesh-babu as their patron."

Times had changed but even now, Prasad said proudly, there were people from Kolkata, Delhi, and even abroad, who often came down to visit his workshop. They wanted him to demonstrate or show Dokra art to them.

"Suppose the final cast is to be the image of an owl," said Prasad, "We take some clay and develop a core which is roughly in that shape. See, how they are doing it." He pointed at a youth fashioning some clay.

"Then we take some beeswax, resin, and nut oil and mix them together. We cover the core with that wax mix. Then we shape and carve it – working out the decorative details. Look over there …," he pointed out some people – an older lot – engrossed in artistic work.

"Over the wax, we put layers of clay which take the form of the wax they are covering. Then we cook the clay. As we do so, the wax melts away and goes out through ducts we have left for the purpose. Once the wax has been drained out, we pour molten brass scrap in. It hardens between the outer surface of the clay core and the inner surface of the layer of clay that has formed the mould for the owl. It will take the form of the owl that we had carved out on the wax mix. Once it is hardened, we will chip off the clay. See, there they are doing it."

Sure enough, there were people chipping off the clay from several delicate lumps. Owls, elephants, and female figurines were emerging in simple but delicate shapes. They were being brushed and made to shine.

Ma went into ecstasies over them. She bought several pieces. Prasad gave Ratna an owl for free.

"My Dokra craft is famous," Prasad began to boast.

"There is a madam from Delhi who buys my pieces in bulk and sells them in a shop she has – a boutique she has in some place called Hauz Khas – have you ever been there?"

"Yes, I have," said Ma, "and probably bought your pieces without knowing they are yours."

Prasad told them that his pieces are displayed there at the Kolkata airport too, in an outlet run by an NGO (non-governmental organization).

"Foreigners too come and buy my pieces. They like my work in Amrika," Prasad gloated.

"We have heard that your pieces are made of special stuff," said Neel.

"What is it?"

Immediately a film came over Prasad Karmakar's shining eyes.

"That is a secret, *dada*", he mumbled, "A trade secret, no, a family secret. As old as that of your hidden treasure."

"Wh-what—how do you know of it?" Ratna gasped.

"Everybody in the village knows of it. Perhaps even elsewhere. It's hidden somewhere around. Why else do you think people make offers to buy your old broken-down place?"

"This is too much!" said Ma and walked off to the car. Carrying armfuls of Dokra-craft, Neel and Ratna too followed.

23

With the Baul Minstrels

Neel was turning the car homewards when his cell phone rang. It was Julian from Amodpur.

An idea struck Neel. From their place at Shalboni village, train had been the right option for going to Amodpur. But from where they had come – to the outskirts of Shalboni – one could drive over. "Wait a bit," he said to Julian over the cell phone.

"Shall we go to Amodpur, Kaki-ma? You have never seen the Bauls perform."

Ma agreed at once. Neel let Julian know. "We are coming over".

Soon they were on their way.

The car passed through a landscape which lost its lush look as it approached Amodpur, it was on the Bengal-Bihar border. They could see the railway curve towards the same place but from a different end. They did not enter the township of Amodpur, though. The Bauls had their *akhrha* (*akhada*, place of performance) in the open spaces that fell before the township started.

A simple canopy had been erected. Under it, several people had gathered. They were bearded and long-haired –mostly men but also women–carrying *ektara*s or single -stringed guitars made of dried gourds. They wore yellow *alkhalla*s (flowing robes) and strings of dried *tulsi* (basil) sprig round their necks. Some wore patchwork robes and had their hair tied up in buns. They all looked pretty happy. At the centre, an elderly Baul was dancing. He had flowing white hair and beard. By his side was a boy – not more than ten – also a Baul strumming his *ektara*.

Ekdin matir bhitore hobe ghar

Re mon amar

Keno bandho dalan-ghar.

One day, it is underground which will be the home for all.

Why erect a mansion this tall!

"Bauls are buried and not cremated," Neel told Ratna. "That is, they are housed underground. Whether buried or cremated in the end, what is the need for people to build tall mansions? Like bodies, they too crumble away. Everything is temporary. That is why the Bauls don't even write their songs. They do not believe in gathering assets and keeping records. They have no fixed homes but are wandering minstrels."

"And here we are so bothered – so bound – so tied-up," said Ratna, "with Ramesh Chowdhuri's mansion and the treasure hidden in it."

Ma called out. "Look, there Julian is singing! There is Tessa, dancing!" Together with them, Neel and Ratna too began to dance. Ma too sat and swayed to the tunes.

They did not feel like going back.

But, of course, they had to.

24

A Revelation

On the way back, they stopped at the local hospital. It was a small one and lacked many facilities. Ramesh Chowdhuri's son Suresh had founded it, and even though it was now a government hospital, a ward still bore his name.

The doctor – the same one who had treated Mita's parents – gave them the good news. Dida had come out of the coma. She was still unfit to meet people.

"Can we just see her from a distance?" asked Neel and the doctor allowed them that.

There she was lying on an iron hospital bed with drips going into her frail veins.

Shrivelled and shrunk, but a survivor!

Everybody felt much better for the rest of the journey. Even Julian and Tessa shared in their relief.

At home Jethi-ma, Jetha and Baba were delighted to hear of Dida's recovery as well as to see Julian and Tessa.

The dinner was fabulous. Ratna was so tired that she fell asleep half-way through it.

Next morning after a breakfast of puffed rice, milk and mashed bananas, Neel and Ratna went to the family elders. They made a clean breast of all that they had found out about the underground passages.

"So irresponsible, Neel, taking Ratna through all that!" thundered Jetha.

"And without even telling us? What made you think that you could do all this by yourself?" Baba sounded incredulous.

"My hands and feet grow cold when I think of you walking about in those dark tunnels while all of us sleeping happily above!" said Jethi-ma.

"How could you do it?" asked Ma, simply.

But then they turned their attention to the tunnels themselves.

"We must go and investigate," said Jetha. "Right now! Neel, you take us along," said Baba. "No, Ratna, you will not come with us."

Ratna was dying to go but Jethi-ma and Ma said a firm, "Not now."

Julian and Tessa were up by now. "Ratna, you keep them company", said Neel. "They are our guests, you know."

"Which way will you take them?" Ratna asked Neel, "Through my room or through the pond?"

"Your room, silly. Can you see us entering through the opening by the pond side? The three of us with the whole village looking on?"

He took his father and uncle up to Ratna's room. Ratna took Julian and Tessa to the living room, and showed them the various artefacts there, collected over generations.

"That statuette of Venus is flawless marble," Julian commented after examining it. "Carved out of a solid block."

"That Brass Buddha needs polishing, but it is exquisite," said Tessa.

Ratna pointed to a terracotta horse. "That's from Bankura, another district in West Bengal."

"Oh, we know that," said Julian. "Bankura horses are famous. No less famous than the terracotta warriors of China."

"However, besides the marble and the brass, the terracotta and that Dokra seems crude," Ratna could not help remarking.

"Folk art seems crude but that is its beauty," Tessa flared up. "Look at their simple, rudimentary lines. They capture the essence of things, unlike the decorative lines of later art patronized by royalty."

25

Old Diaries Again

"Let's look at the old diaries again," suggested Julian. Ratna brought them down and the three of them began to turn the pages again.

"I am concerned about how fast the political scene is changing. As if the First World War was not enough, there seems to be a second one coming up. What funny whiskers that Hitler has! If I ask the barber to shape my whiskers like his, how shall I look? I'll ask Soudamini if I can."

Julian and Tessa smirked.

"The famines that used to occur somewhere or other every year till 1920 or so seem to have stopped. Rainfall is good. No droughts. If only there is no Second World War!" wrote Ramesh Chowdhuri in the year 1938.

"Just as I thought, the Second World War has started. What is more, Governor-General Lord Linlithgow has gone and declared the participation of Indian soldiers in the war without consulting Indians themselves. Protests have started. Ministers are resigning. M. K. Gandhi – everyone calls him Bapuji now–has said that Indian support to the British will be there only if it is there is `transfer of power' at the end of the War – if Britain wins it. Anyway, there is bound to be trouble. Things are going to be shaken up. So, it is just as well that I have all those bunkers, tunnels, and trapdoors made. If there is bombing while I am in the *kachhari*, I can go into the bunker from the trapdoor there. If it bombs while I am in the *andarmahal*, I just have to go to that small room upstairs, and escape through its door."

"That's my room he is referring to", said Ratna.

There was another entry, unrelated to the trend of events.

"Soudamini is getting her special recipes jotted down for daughters-in-law of the future- maybe even grand-daughters-in-law. That is a good idea, considering how women are getting education and employment. What I don't like is that her getting Nayeb-moshai to write the recipes down for her. I offered but she said that my handwriting is not good enough."

Ratna giggled but could not really blame the Soudamini she had never seen, Ramesh Chowdhuri's handwriting was quite atrocious.

Ramesh Chowdhuri had continued to note other events of those times.

One was that to meet military requirements the world over, the government was making heavy purchases of food grains and prices of food grains had started rising.

Another was a reference of the year 1940 to Udham Singh shooting at Michael O'Dwyer Governor of Punjab in order to avenge the Jallianwala Bagh massacre. There was a surprise at the population growing steadily to 389 million as per the 1941 Census.-Ramesh Chowdhuri was aghast as he wrote his diary in 1941. "Japan has entered the Second World War! The import of food grains from Burma and

Siam into India has become difficult. Indian leaders want food exports banned. But in order to meet the demands of the military in different parts of the world, they have no choice but to continue. Prices are rising further."

Ratna opened the diary of 1942.

The Cripps Commission has come to India to decide the terms of the transfer of power Bapuji had negotiated with the British. But the Congress Party is finding them unacceptable.

From 8 August, at the Congress held in Bombay, the land of Shivaji, a new movement has started. It is called the Quit India. "*Angrez, Bharat chhoro!*" is its cry.

In this diary, Ramesh Chowdhuri made a surprising revelation.

"I am trying my hand at poetry. Soudamini does not think much of them, though. Here is a couplet I wrote today:

Jaltungi nodir duiti dhar dhorey

Dhaner shisher pataka sab orey

"Let me see," Ratna quickly translated:

"Paddy fields on by Jaltungi do lie

Waving their stalks, golden flags they fly."

"We can't really call that great talent!" laughed Julian.

The 1943 entries in the diaries were about the Bengal Famine.

"After a respite of more than two decades, there is famine again in the country, but it is a famine of a different kind.

Not because of shortages due to crop failure but because of shortages created by people. Food grain, especially rice, was being imported from Burma and Siam but after Japan entered the War, it has become difficult to get them in the country, while exports continue so as to feed soldiers abroad. Then there are cyclone and floods. Large stocks of food grains are being removed from Bengal to prevent them from getting destroyed or their falling into the hands of enemies. People are hoarding, yes, that is the new term. This is causing a huge exodus of rural population towards Calcutta.

Villagers are selling off their land, plough, cattle, jewellery, utensils, tools, and implements. Then they are leaving their villages and walking towards Calcutta where they know the food is being stored away from them. Every day I get reports of starving villagers reaching there – crying out for gruel. The hoarders there do not open their go-downs to them. It is really the women who are setting up public kitchens and ladling out gruel. Famished people are licking up gruel right from the pavements where it is being poured out. Thousands of people are dying daily on the streets of Calcutta. The official estimate is around three million but I am sure it is more.

Yesterday Nayeb-moshai was giving me such harrowing reports when I felt a shooting pain on the left side of my chest. But, of course, even after I die, my family is well-protected. Apart from the stocked up paddy, I have rubies and emeralds packed and stored secretly within the layers of mother Earth ... now that is a rather poetic way of saying where I have kept them! Let me see if I can put it in rhyme!"

"There, see! The reference to the buried treasure!" Ratna was triumphant.

CHAPTER 6

26
Commotion

There was a commotion upstairs.

Ratna, Julian, and Tessa ran up to Ratna's room.

The door that opened on to the secret passage below and beyond was ajar. Emerging from behind it were Baba, Jetha, Neel and another fellow. It was Moti, the helper at the village provision store owned by moneylender Vishnu. The one whom Ratna had seen at Kusum-dida's place, pressing her for dues at the store. There were still dark circles around his narrow eyes but his mouth with its big white teeth no longer opened in that lopsided grin.

He was bawling.

"I don't know anything, babu. I just do as Vishnu *mahajan* tells me."

Jetha had held him in an iron grip.

Baba explained, "Found him carrying two pesticide containers away from that place."

"Vishnu *mahajan* asked me to do so. They are his."

"What are they doing here then? This house is not his, is it?"

"No, babu, but it is his godown!"

"What! So, Vishnu has been using our basement or whatever as his godown!"

"Yes, you have never said `no'!"

"That's because I never knew about it!" yelled Jetha.

"Nor I," said Baba and Neel in one voice.

The three of them had been unaware of the existence of the basement with its secret passages in and out. The local moneylender had come upon it and had used it as a storage space for various items that he could not store in his provision shop. Especially those that did not have ISI marks and did not conform to norms of quality.

"I'll hand you over to the police," shouted Jetha, his face red.

Moti howled louder. He fell at the feet of Jethi-ma, who had come in with Ma.

She softened towards Moti.

"He is just Vishnu *Mahajan*'s servant. Why take it out on him? Neel, call up the *Mahajan* and ask him for an explanation."

Neel was sent to get Vishnu Poddar while the rest of them trooped down to the living room.

Moti, who had never been there, looked around in wonder even as he stood cowering before all of them.

"Vishnu *mahajan* refused to come," Neel announced on returning after half-an-hour or so.

"These are not the old feudal times when the landlord could summon up his subjects to his *kachhar*i. That is what he said," Neel reported.

"You know, I thought someone might say so soon," whispered Tessa in Ratna's ears.

"Besides, he denied that those pesticides are his or that he ever asked Moti to store them there. He says he has nothing to do with them and I am just piling it on him because I am mad about organic farming. Yes, that's what he said. Mad!"

"Well, Neel, so am I," Julian said soothingly, "organically mad." Neel cooled down and grinned.

"It's the police then," said Jetha, looking even redder. "Let them come and pick this fellow up. He has been caught red-handed trespassing on our property."

"No," said Baba. "Don't call the police in just yet. Let me go with Bhupen and tackle Vishnu Poddar. After all, Neel is just a kid."

Ratna thought Neel-dada looked indignant and was about to protest. She also saw Julian wink at him as if to say `hold it'.

Baba went out. "I'll get Bhupen on the way. So that Vishnu cannot deny his connection with the pesticides stacked in our premises."

"Let's all go to the *kachhari* then", said Jetha, "now that Vishnu has accused us of being feudal!"

Jetha and Neel took Moti to the *kachhari* with them.

Julian and Tessa said that the whole thing had really made them feel very, very hungry. "Come and have some *jalkhaba*r," said Jethi-ma. Ma and Ratna followed her to the kitchen.

27

Vishnu Poddar's Audacity

Although *jal* means simply water and *khabar* meant food, *jalkhabar* is usually the word used for breakfast or tiffin in Bengal, usually, it is *luchi begun-bhaja, or luchi-alu-bhaj*a (puffed-up *puri*s of flour served with fried slices of brinjal or potato).

Jethi-ma quickly piled their plates with *luchi-begun-bhaja.*

Half-way through it, Mita came along.

Her father had gone with Ratna, she had felt that she must- simply must – see what is happening there.

"Mita, sit down and have some *jalkhaba*r," said Jethi-ma.

By the time they had finished, the car had come back with Baba, Kaka, and Vishnu *mahajan*. Ratna saw it drive past the mansion to the *kachhari.* They trooped down to the *kachhari* through a shaded but open corridor that led there.

No, Jetha was not seated upon the old Jomidar's couch so close to the trap-door through which Ratna had fallen.

He sat on a simple bench at the entrance of the hall. There were a couple of benches there, probably been kept there once for some people to sit and wait while the Jomidar dealt with others.

Baba, Bhupen-kaka, and an unknown man sat on these. Moti crouched at the feet of the unknown man – who must, therefore, be Vishnu Poddar, the *Mahajan*, a middle-aged man in a loud, orange T-shirt that barely covered his paunch. He had heavy-lidded eyes and pink, rotten gums.

He stood up and with a show of respect, bowed to Jethi-ma and Ma.

They sat on a bench, and Jetha began to speak to Vishnu Poddar, the village merchant and money-lender.

"Poddar, this is not about feudal attitudes. I called you because you have been trespassing on my property. You have been using my basement as a godown of sorts, that too for sub-standard stuff you shouldn't be selling anyway."

"Dwijesh-babu, you didn't even know you had that basement. Why be so upset at someone putting it to good use?" Vishnu laughed in Jetha's face.

Jetha clutched at the bench he was sitting on but kept his cool.

"Poddar, whether or not we knew we had it or not, that basement is part of our house and part of our property."

"Would you like some rent for it? and keep the matter quiet?"

"Perhaps, had you offered the rent to start with and be open about what you are storing there. Now that is out of the question," said Jetha.

"I completely agree," said Baba.

"Now, just clear the basement and stop selling those pesticides," Bhupen-kaka continued in the same vein. Vishnu turned his glare upon him.

"Why do you come in, Bhupen-babu? What business is it of yours? Besides, you were happy enough to purchase it in the first place. What happened? Didn't you like its taste?"

Bhupen got up as if to deal Vishnu a blow but Baba pulled him back.

"Poddar!" Jetha commanded, "Clear up the basement within an hour with that Moti of yours. Otherwise, we call the police."

"—and complain to the Bureau of Indian Standards as well as environmentalists," added Baba.

"Threatening me?" Vishnu spat out, "Small people like me, who have lived for generations in a small way while big men like you have flourished? All right, I will clear out of the basement. You can make me. But can you make that couple clear off?"

"Which couple – what are you talking about?" Jetha spluttered.

"As if you don't know! Those two from the city–to whom you are selling the whole of your property, basement and all? Can you stop them from doing so?"

"Why should we?" asked Baba as Jetha suddenly seemed to fall silent, "They are paying us good money – they are not doing anything underhand like you."

Vishnu laughed.

"Aren't they? Paying you a mere pittance and getting their hands on the buried treasure. Isn't that underhand?"

"What is all this, Poddar-moshai?" said Baba, politely adding `*moshai*' (a colloquial form of *mahashaya*) to the surname of the village money-lender. "They have offered us a good amount."

"Isn't what they have offered too good an amount? For a ramshackle old place like this? Have you thought why they are making an offer for it?"

"Well, it is a good place for building a hotel which is what they said they want to build."

"And what do you think, Neel-babu?" Vishnu Poddar turned to Neel. "Soil that has got water, soil that's good for food crops and fruit…is it to be used for a hotel? I am only a *mahajan* – a small village moneylender. Even I feel sad at the idea. This is also my village after all."

"Stop diverting from the issue, Poddar," Jetha's voice rang out again, "You have been using our premises illegally. Vacate at once or I will call the police."

"That's scary! Jomidar babu Dwijesh Chowdhuri" sniggered Vishnu Poddar. "It will make me run, like my great-uncle Shyamu! And get killed on the railway tracks."

Ratna gave a huge, big start.

This man, a descendant of the Shyamu she had heard about and almost seen!

No wonder he had a grudge against their family.

28

A Break

Although Vishnu was defiant and disrespectful, Vishnu *Mahajan* assured them that he would make Moti remove the pesticide containers, taking them out through the opening that was near the pond. Come to think of it, it had been a convenient godown for them, thought Ratna. Before Vishnu himself cleared out of the sight of Jetha and Baba, he dropped a bombshell.

"That old woman – that grand-daughter of the Nayeb who cannot even pay for what she buys from me – I know who tried to kill her and why."

"Who was it?" everybody asked him. But he closed his heavy-lidded eyes and smiled silently, baring his pink gums.

Afterwards, Neel himself blocked the opening of the tunnel with some loose bricks and broken marble chips. Julian helped him. Jetha did not want to call a professional bricklayer or grille-maker. It would just make a bigger story of the whole thing, he felt.

"And Somesh, I think we must cancel the deal with those two. Or at least stall it."

"They have not yet got back after the search of the documents –," Baba began.

"But whatever they get back with, I am having doubts about the deal," said Jetha.

Jethi-ma endorsed this. "Somesh-Thakur-po, old and inconvenient as I feel Chowdhuri Niwas is, I don't think we should be in such a hurry to sell it."

Today Ma too put her arms round Jethi-ma. "Didi, you are right."

To get a break from all this talk, all of them went to the open stretch at the top of the mansion. It was really pleasant and peaceful.

"Once here on the roof it's difficult to remember that there is so much complication below," said Ratna, remembering the labyrinth underground.

A soft, wet breeze wafted across, carrying the message that monsoon was not far behind. The season of mangoes and jamuns was going to change.

Neel rang the hospital from his cell phone. Kusum-dida was being released from the hospital tomorrow.

"Ma, should I get her and drop her to her place?"

Jethi-Ma had asked him to bring her there itself.

"Who will look after her in the hut she lives in? With those rats in the corner, it is not safe for anyone. Besides, whoever hit her will get to know that she is back. He may try again."

"But here ...?" Khiri, the maid, sounded shocked. "This is the mansion of Jomidars."

"All the more reason," commanded Jethi-ma with pursed lips, "we should care for the old Nayeb's daughter. Now go and clean the small room next to the entrance."

"Jethi-ma, you're looking like an Indian goddess!" said Tessa as she came up. Ratna agreed admiringly.

The evening was falling. The birds were returning to their nests on the trees. A few bats were flying back to the ceilings and alcoves of the mansion.

"Shall I sing a Baul song that I picked up at Amodpur?" asked Julian. "I was told that it is by the great fakir Lalan."

Sab lokey koy Lalan ki jaat ei sansare

Lalan koy jaater bichar dekhlam na ei nagare

(Everyone asks what caste Lalan belongs to and why,

` I do not see any distinctions of caste', says Lalan in reply.)

"Thank God for the Lalan Fakirs of this world!" said Tessa, "We seem to be bothered all the time about who is rich and who is poor, who is high-up and who is not. The Bauls are above all that, and free."

Julian sang some more. A full moon raised its head above the sleepy trees. They went down and went through Ramesh Chowdhuri's diaries again.

29

The Last Page of the Diary

"See, this is an entry of 1944," Ratna pointed at a diary that looked relatively new.

The Azad Hind Fauj (Indian National Army, INA), under the leadership of Subhash Chandra Bose, has made a bold bid for freedom. It is reported that his soldiers had reached Imphal and even hoisted our national flag there. But now it is in retreat and Subhash Chandra Bose has gone underground.

In late August, Ramesh Chowdhuri wrote:

There is a report that on a flight from Japan, an air crash has ended Subhash's life and aspirations. There are contrary reports as well.

A 1944 entry said: The British has set up an enquiry commission into the Bengal Famine and has even set up a Planning and Development Department. Too late, I think, to make Indians give up our cry for freedom.

Hitler has committed suicide in a bunker below the ground. What an end! But it means that the War is ending and I will never have to use my tunnels. Well, they are rather good and I am glad I got them made.

In early 1945 there was the brief entry, "Soudamini has passed away. I am devastated."

On 24 October 1945, he wrote: "United Nations has been formed and India has been made a member. ...My chest hurts. With Soudamini gone, I feel rather lonely. Is that why my chest hurts?..."

Ah, there is the 1947 diary.

"I was so unhappy and ill in between that I had stopped writing diaries but now I am better and feel like writing again. India is now Independent. It happened like this. The British had proposed partitioning of India. On January 6, 1947, the All India Congress Committee accepted this proposal (by a majority vote of 99 against 52). On March 24, Lord Mountbatten (great-grandson of Queen Victoria) was installed as the *last* Viceroy of India. On July 18 the India Independence Act was passed by the British Parliament. Two countries were formed out of the one country."

"I feel sick at the reports of how this has affected the lives of people. I am already sick, so I will not dwell on that. From 17th August British troops have started leaving India in shiploads. The French have willingly ceded their territories to India but the Portuguese are hanging on. They were the first to come to India and are likely to be the last to leave. But now what of the changes which Indians bring to India? Will life be the same for the likes of me or will it change? That is what worries me."

Either he was too devastated to write more in 1948-49, or those diaries were lost.

In 1950 he wrote again: "On 15 March, an arm of the Central Government called Yojana Ayog or Planning Commission has been established with Prime Minister Jawaharlal Nehru as the Chairman. The planning is to be done in units of five years and the first one is said to be focusing on agricultural growth. Suresh, who is studying in Presidency College, is pretty excited about it. But Nayeb-moshai is not. I feel detached."

"In 1951, our great grandfather was quite worried," said Ratna as she read further. "Nayeb-moshai has heard, and he usually hears right, that India is going to introduce what they are calling `land reform'. That means the land tenure system introduced as early as 1793 by Lord Cornwallis might be overhauled. But is such a thing possible? The more I think about it, the more I have chest pains. But I shall go on holding my *kachhari* as usual. Let us see what happens."

A few pages later there was another entry that caught Ratna's attention.

"Today I lost a faithful servant. Haru *lathiyal*, my Haru, who has guarded my fields, my gardens, my ponds as though they were his own. He had caught a village lad – named Shyamu, they said–fishing where he should not. Haru had brought him to the *kachhari*. I had just dealt with Gupi Mohan and Razak Mian, and now it was this Shyamu's turn.

But he had broken away from Haru and run away, towards the railway station, probably hoping to jump onto a train and escape. My Haru ran out after him and caught up with him. But a train passed by just then killed them both, and robbing me of my loyal *lathiyal*."

शालबनी
Shalboni

Well, Ratna thought, if great-grandpa was not bothered about a young kid from his own village, at least he was bothered by the loss of one who died serving him.

"Nayeb-moshai told me today that it was not just for fishing in our pond that Haru had caught hold of that boy Shyamu. He had found Shyamu ferreting about and peeping into the mouth of the tunnel leading out of the basement. In other words, that Shyamu had almost discovered the secret passages under the mansion. So, I am not going to hire any hands to clear the pond up. Let the water hyacinths grow and cover up the tunnel mouth."

"This explains why Ramesh Chowdhuri let the pond fall into disuse," said Tessa.

Ratna continued to read from the diary.

"Before I die – which may be any day- the chest pains are worse despite all the doctor's prescriptions – I must give Suresh my message. It's quite a nice rhyme, actually. Perhaps I should have been a poet rather than a landlord – like Rabindranath Tagore."

"Huh!" said Neel. The others began to laugh. Only Ratna looked serious.

"It's torn from here," she held up the page for all to see.

Subdued and sobered, they went down for dinner.

One of the items at dinner was stuffed capsicum. The capsicums were from Neel's fields and, of course, all organic. Under Jethi-Ma's instructions, Khiri had worked wonders with them.

"Why are you looking so thoughtful?" Tessa asked Ratna.

"I was thinking," Ratna replied, "Spicy potato with thick capsicum skin is just like… Inside, the earth is packed with jewel and gem. Why take the words 'inside the earth' to mean underground? Maybe the underground passages were just air-raid precautions and nothing more? The valuables are stuffed elsewhere, within some earthenware? Some pot in the larder? Some jar in the kitchen? "

"You know, if that is how Ramesh Chowdhuri hid his valuables, the first thing is to keep them safe within the mansion," said Julian.

CHAPTER 7

30

The Offer Refused

Quite early next morning, Neel went out as he had to fetch Kusum-dida from the hospital. Mita came over as she wanted to be there when Kusum-dida came.

A little while later, the shining blue Audi whizzed in once again before the Chowdhuri Niwas. Once again two people got out and stood to look the mansion.

The young man was in a white T-shirt while the young lady in trousers and a top of *khadi*.

Jetha and Baba received them and took them to the living room. Khiri came and offered them water in polished glasses of brass, as was the custom of the house.

Ratna, Mita, Tessa, and Julian hung around in another part of the same room. They were dying of curiosity as to what would happen! Once Khiri had served them tea, Jethi-Ma and Ma too sat down with the guests.

"Well, Mr Chowdhuri," the lady addressed Jetha. "We are done with our search of the property papers. All the papers are in order and we want to buy the property and take possession immediately."

"I am afraid that is not possible," said Jetha politely, "We need more time to think about the deal."

"In fact, we are thinking of **not** going ahead with the deal," said Baba.

"What? But then why did you give us the papers to search?" exclaimed the lady.

"You were all for it last time, what happened?" the man asked.

"Yes, but we have second thoughts," said Jetha, still being polite.

"We can raise our offer," said the lady, "In fact, we can double it."

Ratna saw Jetha raise his eyebrows at that. But he smiled the next instant and said, "That is what is making us have our second thoughts. If it is such an attractive piece of property then perhaps we should not be disposing of it."

The man changed his tracks and said, "Mr Chowdhuri, we came all the way from Delhi for this. You encouraged us. You led us on. Now you can't simply say you are having second thoughts."

"Look here," said Jetha, as politely as ever, " We did not sign any Agreement of Sale with you or make any legal commitment. I am not bound in any way to sell our ancestral property."

"But, why backtrack now?" the lady asked, looking appealingly to Ma and Jethi-ma. But Ratna saw her glance sweep over the furniture and the carpet, the marble and the brass, the earthenware and the Dokra. It was as if she was taking stock of everything.

"It is a very good offer we are making. Sell us the whole property, furniture and books, papers and artefacts intact, and you will have cash like you have never see."

"We need more time," said Ma.

"No, we need no more time," Jethi-ma corrected her. "We have decided we are not selling".

"Oh, you village people!" the lady seemed exasperated, "You are all the same."

"What do you mean?" Ma butted in even as the lady stopped midway in her statement.

"Nothing! But please Mrs Chowdhuri, ask your husband and brother-in-law to reconsider –"

Just then there was the sound of a car arriving and the main door opening. Neel was back with Kusum-dida. Unaware of there being visitors, he raised the curtain of the living room with his right hand, supporting Kusum-dida with his left.

Ma and Jethi-ma got up and began walking towards her. But before they could welcome her in, the frail old woman took one look at the visitors – who were face to face with her–and shrieked loudly.

31

The Assaulters Exposed

"Aaagh!" Her incoherent cry trembled through the living room. She pointed her shrivelled index at the two visitors and collapsed in Neel's arms.

At the sight of her, the visitors froze for a moment and then tried to move towards the door. But Ratna quickly caught the lady's hand and Tessa stood blocking her way. Julian had gripped the man and Jethi-ma came and blocked his escape route.

For in that one instant it had become clear to everyone that it was they who had hit Kusum-dida. The *mahajan* must have known this all along. He may even have been party to it!

Neel led Kusum-dida into a chair. Ma went over and sprinkled some water on her face –water that had originally been offered to the visitors.

"Why are they here? Ask them to go away!" Kusum-dida opened her eyes and began to stutter.

The lady immediately caught on to this and said, "She seems disturbed. Is she mentally stable? Who is she?"

The man piped in, "Anyway, as she is saying, let us go. We will come another time." "No, Sir," said Baba, finally recovered after the first few bewildered moment, "Never again. We'll settle the matter once for all." He latched the main door so that no one could escape. "Neel, call the police, " ordered Jetha.

"I told you to keep your cool that day and not hit her," the lady hissed.

"Shhh—you keep your own cool now," the man hissed back.

Ratna put her arms round Kusum-dida and asked to explain, however slowly.

"Those two came to my place earlier. They wanted me to sell it to them, along with its land. I said `no'. Where will I go, selling off what my ancestors have left me?"

So that is why, Ratna realized, when her uncle and father had cried off the deal, the lady had exclaimed: You village people, you are all the same.

"True enough," Jethi-ma was saying to Kusum-dida.

"But these people would not let me be", Dida went on. "They were offering me lakhs through that Vishnu Poddar. Money, they tempted me with money in exchange for land– the soil of my own village. I said `no' to Vishnu also."

"Don't listen to all this," the man said, his T-shirt sopping wet with sweat, "She is an old woman, and has had a concussion."

Immediately Ratna saw him bite his tongue.

At once Jetha said: "And how do you know that? We did not give you that piece of information, did we?"

The man began to look here and there as if wanting to run away.

Kusum-dida had a sip of water and continued:

"What puzzled me was that they were willing to pay for the stacks of papers that were there on the floor. Old documents, diaries, and notebooks from long ago. They were precious to me. But why would be precious to anyone else? Why should total strangers want to pay for them? So, I hung on to them."

"That was brave of you, Dida," said Ratna. "Neel-dada and I had told you a lot about what money can do. But there's something money cannot do, and that is buying what is not for sale. One's guts. One's spirit."

Kusum-dida frowned as if she could not understand. But she went on.

"That afternoon when they came, they badgered me and I said, "No, no, no for the last time." Then I saw that man pick up a huge pile of papers, raise it, and bring it down upon my head."

"So that was what you were hit on the head with. A thick wad of files and ledgers!"

The man decided to open his mouth and come clean.

"It was done in a fit of temper but knocked her out completely. We then picked up the papers and made off with them, latching the door from outside. The Audi had been waiting outside the village."

"Why, what did you want with the papers?" asked Neel.

"They may have contained clues to the treasure we all know is here", the man looked up at last, "That old woman's father was the Nayeb of Jomidar Ramesh Chowdhuri. He may have put it there, among other papers, all of which his daughter had inherited That is why we had offered to buy her entire house along with the papers."

"Just as you offered to buy our place with all its stuff included?" asked Jetha in a stunned voice, "All that talk of building a hotel here was nonsense. You are after our family inheritance!"

"Leave it for us to find'" Ratna felt like shouting at the man, "Neel-dada and I can do it."

The police arrived and took the couple away on charges of assaulting Kusum-dida. "We will soon be out on bail," they said as they went. "There is no case against us."

Once they were gone, Jethi-ma and Ma busied themselves in making Kusum-dida comfortable in her bed. Mita's parents came over. Baba was glad to recount the events to Bhupen-kaka. Kusum-dida was happy to have Mita's mother tending to her.

32

'Bagging' the Treasure

Ratna, Neel, Mita, Julian, and Tessa remained in the living room, chatting about the revelations of the last couple of hours. Jethi-ma came in, carrying a big brass platter of home-made chips (*alu-bhaja*) for them.

She placed it on a glass-topped table crowded with artefacts. "Munch these as you do your sorting and packing."

Ratna did not let her go. "Sit down among us and chat. Tell everybody what you told me about Ramesh Chowdhuri's last moments."

"I was not yet married then. But I have heard the account later from my father-in-law, Suresh Chowdhuri. It was in the year 1952. Ramesh Chowdhuri was in the *kachhari* with Nayeb-moshai and a few villagers. My father-in-law had been away in Kolkata but he came back at mid-day by the Bengal Beauty. He made straight for the *kachhari* with the morning's newspaper in hand. A new law had been passed. Jomidari had been abolished in Bengal. This news triggered a heart attack and Ramesh Chowdhuri passed away. Just before he did, he tried to give my father-in-law a last message. In the panic of that moment, Suresh Chowdhuri could only glance at it. He put it down somewhere and never saw it again. Ramesh Chowdhuri's last message was lost. My father-in-law could only remember a few words that had caught his eyes even as he put it away. *Matir bhitor rattan anek* ..and such like. That's what he had passed down to us upon his death. The mansion, some land and those mysterious lines.' .....Coming!" she suddenly broke off, "There's your Jetha calling me. Enjoy the chips!"

She got up and went away.

They reached for the platter of chips on the crowded table. Tessa knocked against a Dokra elephant and it fell on a patch where the marble was showing through the frayed carpet. They picked the elephant up but noticed that the trunk had broken.

"Look what I have done," Tessa exclaimed.

"It's tougher than one thinks," said Ratna. "See, only the trunk of the elephant is broken. The rest of the body is still intact."

Tessa bent down to pick the elephant up minus its trunk. At that precise moment, Ratna too bent down to pick the trunk up. They collided. The elephant fell from Tessa's hands and this time, broke into pieces, the belly separated from the legs.

"I am so sorry," Tessa sounded appalled.

"Well, it was a pretty old piece," Ratna tried to save her from feeling embarrassed. "But don't worry, there are others. At least now we know exactly what an elephant's belly contains. At least a Dokra elephant's belly"

"Do we?"

Neel's voice sounded strange.

"Look, all of you, just look!"

Pieces of metal and clay scattered on the floor.

And something else.

A sparkling something.

A green something.

A stone.

A jewel.

Ratna shrieked. Jethi-ma and Ma came running.

Ratna pointed at the floor.

Jethi-ma picked up the stone and examined it in the light. Her face muscles began to work. She could not get her words out.

But Ma could and she declared, "*Panna.*"

"An emerald," Ratna translated for Julian and Tessa.

In a faint, wondering voice, Jethi-ma began to recite;

Matir bhitor ratan anek bhawra

Shakto holo segulo bar kawra.

"*Matir bhitor*, that's right! To make a Dokra artefact, one does use clay, that is, *mati,*" Ratna exclaimed. "And an emerald put within a Dokra piece can certainly be called *ratan,* that is *matir bhitor bhawra.*"

"Like the stuffed capsicum you were thinking about!" added Tessa.

"Don't forget the *anek* part. *Matir bhitor rattan anek* . So there are more!" Neel's brain was working fast. "Other Dokra pieces may also contain jewels. That's why Jomidar Ramesh Chowdhuri patronized Dokra craft although he could afford sculptures of marble and brass."

"But then there was also something about water..*jodi bhasao jale.* My father-in-law could remember that very clearly. That does not tie up with this, does it?"

Everyone had to agree. That part of the message still made no sense.

Jethi-ma shook herself, picking the emerald up, she took it away for safekeeping. Ma gathered up the broken pieces herself, saying: "I don't want Khiri and the other maids to guess anything while they are clearing the pieces."

Stunned as they were, Ma and she had to go back to their household work, especially with Kusum-dida under their care.

Ratna, Mita, Tessa, Julian, and Neel took down all the Dokra crafts from the various places.

"Short of breaking an item," said Mita, "there's no way of finding if it contains a gem. Such a pity!"

"No, there might be baggage scanners and X-ray machines which can do the job. Like the Rapiscan ones in metro stations, airports, courts, and even some malls," Ratna said.

"They will detect black spots where gems are embedded. Many artefacts will then be spared."

"So, let's pack all the Dokra artefacts into boxes or bags which we can take to Kolkata and Delhi and get scanned," Tessa suggested.

"Why don't we try the hospital here?" said Ratna. "See if their X-ray machines can help?"

"Good idea! Then we can just take a few Dokra pieces there and get them X-rayed, provided the hospital authorities agree!" said Julian. "I'll talk to them," said Neel. "With Kusum-dida and Bhupen-kaka getting hospitalized, I have got to know several doctors there."

"Besides, they are locals and know about us," added Ratna. "One of the hospital wings bears the name of Ramesh Chowdhuri. Surely, they will allow the experiment, at least if Jetha speaks to them."

"If not, we will hire a scanner or X-ray machine from somewhere…," Neel said.

"You know what," he continued, "Prasad Karmakar's finding a special ingredient for his Dokra work may just be a hype. A publicity stunt. What he does is to put a stone or pebble within the earth so as to make it stronger. He does not know how this started – how Ramesh Chowdhuri asked one of his forefathers to do it in order to hide his gems and gold. He does it as tricks of the trade – and instead of hiding it, uses it as a publicity gimmick.

"Could be…why not?" Tessa agreed.

Julian suggested they also pack all the papers that were lying around, especially the diaries. Already much is lost, such as the ones that were lying in Kusum-dida's place. But those that are there may still be salvaged.

"They will be of value to researchers for economic history of India," he said.

"But first let's put Dokra pieces and put them in a big bag. Then we can take them to the hospital tomorrow to see if Ratna's idea works," Tessa said.

"I am sure that fat owl has a fat gem in it", said Mita, pointing to a piece. "What about that elephant there?" Julian said.

"Pack them carefully, with soft rags in between," Ratna instructed, "We don't want them to break."

They started working with enthusiasm.

CHAPTER 8

33

The Last Act

Once they had finished bagging the Dokra artefacts, they made their way to the *kachhari*. There might be some artefacts and papers to be picked up from there as well and packed. As soon as Ratna entered, she saw ……

…..an elderly man with fine features and fine silk lay among cushions of various sizes and shapes. He looked tired and weak. Before him, there was a low stool – a foot-rest. A hawk-nosed man in a turban sat beside him on a lower chair. By his side, there was a pile of papers and diaries.

Villagers kept approaching the couch. The entrance still had guards. Neel, Julian, Tessa, and Mita, where were they?

Ratna found herself alone, facing a scene that is more than six decades old.

"Jishnu, I hear you are charging high interest from the peasants. Much higher than what the banks are charging."

"They get it more easily from me," Jishnu replied. Vishnu had certainly inherited his looks, "That is why we *mahajans* are still in business."

"Baba-moshai (Respected Father)!"

The guards at the entrance quickly moved apart. A young man rushed in. He looked so very like Ramesh Chowdhuri that Ratna instantly knew: this was grandfather Suresh.

"Baba-moshai!" he waved, "It's out in the papers! They have passed the West Bengal Land Reform Act. *Jomidari* is a thing of the past!" Ramesh Chowdhuri immediately clutched at his heart, "You mean I am no longer Jomidar Ramesh Chowdhuri?"

"No, Baba."

"Nayeb mosh…" he tried to say, "My di.."

The Nayeb handed some diaries.

Ramesh Chowdhuri began to sputter. No one could make out what he was saying. His eyes began to roll and he began to choke.

"Call the *daktar* (doctor) babu!" The Nayeb ordered the guards. Some people stood stunned, some ran here and there.

"Baba, don't take on so because there is no *jomidari* any more!" His son tried to comfort him. Ramesh Chowdhuri shook his head violently and stretched his hand at a diary. Ramesh Chowdhuri pulled at the page with all his dying strength. It got torn. Ramesh seemed to be trying to hand it over to his son. Suresh took it from his father and began to read it aloud.

Matir bhitor ratan anek bhawra

Shakto holo segulo bar kawra.

Sonadana hiremanik jwale

Rukkho mati jodi bhasao jale.

What nonsense was this, and at this hour too!

He made a puzzled face gesture and tossed it away carelessly into a sheaf of papers that lay there. Then he turned anxiously to his father. But he had closed his eyes and did not even look at his son. The Nayeb felt his pulse and stood back. The doctor arrived and shook his head. People crowded around them. More and more people began to rush in. Soon the scene was one of utter chaos.

Ratna saw a hand steal towards the torn scrap of paper that contained the message Ramesh Chowdhuri wanted to give his son and heir.

It was the Nayeb's hand.

"Bah, Nayeb-moshai bah! Stealing already!" a voice exclaimed.

"Jishnu, hold your tongue!"

The voice belonged to Jishnu Poddar, father of Vishnu Poddar, "Not unless you help me hold it. Nayeb-moshai, I saw you steal that last message of our *jomidar babu*!"

"Ratna, Ratna! What's wrong with you!" Ratna came back to the present with a bang. Neel, Julian, Tessa, and Mita were staring at her.

"We thought you had gone bonkers!" giggled Tessa

"You looked as if you were watching a TV show," Neel commented.

"I got worried," muttered Mita.

"I have to tell you something," said Ratna. "Only, let's get out of here."

34

In the Fresh Air

Sitting in the fresh air under the jackfruit and jamun trees by the pond, Ratna told them about her first experiences in the *kachhari*.

She had seen a scene from the past enacted before her eyes when *jomidar* Ramesh Chowdhuri, the *nayeb* by his side, lorded over villagers like Gupi Mohan and Razak Mian. It was clear that the secret underground passages had already been made. The village lad, Shyamu, had chanced upon them while fishing in his pond. That is why it was such a serious offence for Haru *lathiyal* to haul him up before the *jomidar* and go after him when he ran away from the *kachhari*, both losing their lives as a consequence.

"Ghosts!" gasped Mita. Her *kajal*-ringed eyes were round.

"You must have imagined it all," Tessa wrinkled her nose.

"But, Tessa, that Shyamu could not have been imagination," said Neel, "The stationmaster also talked of it-"

"And when he did, I felt strange –not scared just strange –", Ratna tried to explain, "For I had seen part of it – when Shyamu broke away from Haru and ran away…"

"You could have told me about it," Neel sounded a little offended.

"I was scared you would think it is silly," said Ratna, "and say it is all my imagination."

"But after what you said today, I won't," said Neel, "It is the same as Ma's account of Ramesh Chowdhuri's death and is in tune with whatever we found in the diaries."

"But then do we also take it that it was the Nayeb – Kusum-dida's father–who stole that crucial piece of paper containing the clues to what Ramesh Chowdhuri had hidden?" Julian asked.

"And that Jishnu *mahajan* – Vishnu *mahajan*'s father – saw him do it?" Tessa spoke up.

Neel ventured further and built up an outline of what could have happened.

Perhaps that gave Jishnu *mahajan* some power over the Nayeb. He began to ask for hush-money. The Nayeb paid up. For he thought that the slip of paper would lead him to a far greater wealth. He began to carry important documents to his place and sift through them. Now that the *jomidari* was gone, Suresh Chowdhuri must have dismissed him. So, on the one hand, he had lost his pay and the power and prestige that came with it. On the other, he was being blackmailed by the village moneylender who was using his hush-money to become a shopkeeper. He bought a piece of land near the pond – because he had got wind of a secret passage leading out to it from the mansion. He set his provision-shop there. Meanwhile, the Nayeb fell more and more into poverty. His daughter – that is Kusum-dida – got widowed and came to live with him. He looked but could never find the wealth. Finally, he died, leaving only a small hut for his daughter and huge stacks of paper. Jishnu too died, possibly telling son Vishnu to look for the secret passage. Vishnu had looked, and even found one end of it. He had put that part to good use, making it a godown for his sub-standard and suspect products.

Neel stopped and bit into a jamun that had fallen into his lap. Actually, the season for jamuns was over. Only a few remained on the tree. A wind had started picking up – and that is why a few jamuns had fallen down.

Just then, some day-labourers passed by with spades and other tools on their shoulders. Why they were stopping by the pond and moving the heap of dried-up hyacinths. Why, they were going towards the mouth of the passage. Why, they were hitting at it!

35

A Thunderous Clash

"What do you think you are doing?" Neel threw away the jamun and advanced towards them.

One of them replied boldly: "We are widening the mouth of the passage so that it is easier to take things in and out of the godown at the end of it. Vishnu babu asked us."

"But he has no right to!" said Neel.

"He does!" said Moti, running out of the shop at the other end of the pond. "His goods are there."

"But Baba asked him to remove them. He has no right to keep them there! Moti, you were also there!"

"Well, we are not going to remove them", said Moti cockily. "Vishnu-babu said so."

"As long as they have their goods there," Julian explained, "they have some right of possession. You can fight it out in court but at the moment they are there. So, they are going to use it to widen the mouth of the passage."

"But why?" asked Ratna.

"To search for the wealth, that they think is there still!" answered Julian. "It's their last bid for it!"

In all this, the labourers had struck quite a few blows at the mouth of the tunnel and widened it. They were strong blows, struck at the very foundations of the mansion.

The main door opened. Jetha and Baba came hurrying out.

"What's all this?" said Jetha. Baba took it in at one glance and took out his cell phone. "I'll call the police".

"You may call the police. You may call the army. But we are not going to budge," Vishnu Poddar stood his ground. "*Chal re*! Go on!" he called out to the labourers.

A gleaming sword split the sky. Moments later came the war-cry of thunder.

A thousand spears of rain came and pierced the bare backs of the labourers, forcing them to abandon their work and scatter away … Vishnu and Moti ran towards their shop, and the others to the mansion.

The jackfruit, the mango, the jamun, the papaya… all the trees shook their head in protest. But the storm grew stronger and stronger. The rain-clouds did not lighten.

A tin roof from somewhere flew off. A mud-wall somewhere collapsed.

"So, this is the Indian monsoon," Julian exclaimed in wonder.

"An experience in itself," cried Tessa.

CHAPTER 9

36

The Rain That Would Not Go Away

All afternoon it rained, and all evening. The roads first became muddy and then turned into small streams.

The torrents lessened a little towards nightfall. Frogs began to croak at the pond.

"Mita, you stay the night at our place," Ratna suggested.

"Yes," Jethi-Ma said, "Don't dream of going home." In any case, Mita's mother, who was there with Kusum-dida readily agreed.

"But Baba.. ", began Mita. "He's alone."

"Oh your Baba, he will manage!" her mother said.

"We won't let you go home now", Ratna put her arm around her.

The rain gathered fresh force. Doors and windows began to slam in distant parts of the house. The electricity was cut off, came back, and went off again. Khiri brought big hurricane lamps and put them here and there.

Nobody felt like going through the open corridor and courtyard towards the kitchen or the dining area. Khiri served them dinner in the living room. They sat on couches and chairs with food piled up before them on the various tables.

The rain continued, sometimes slow, sometimes torrential. The wind rose and fell, howling and whimpering. There were frequent flashes of lightning.

"What a day for Kusum-dida to return!" said Ratna.

"Even though her father the Nayeb may have been a greedy and disloyal man," said Neel, "I am glad she is back."

"Let's forget all that," said Jetha, "Let's also get over that row with Vishnu." Baba seconded him and said, "Let's have a song."

Mita sang a song by Rabindranath Tagore:

" *Aj jharo jharo bari jhare bhara badorey*

Akashbhanga akul dhara kothao na dhorey-ey-ey !"

(There is no place on earth to contain

The passionate outpouring of the monsoon rain…)

Afterwards, Ratna took Mita to her own room. Unfamiliar as the bed was, Mita fell asleep pretty fast. But Ratna lay drowsily for a long time, listening to the rain. After a while, she too fell asleep.

37

Past Midnight

It was past midnight. There was such an ear-splitting thunder that Ratna started out of her sleep. The window had opened and rain was getting in. Ratna got out of the bed to close it. She had to struggle with the strong wind but she did it. It was then that she felt a strange sensation–her ankles were wet. Why, she was ankle-deep in water!

Cold, stinking and brown, it was rushing in from below the wooden door at the back of her room leading into the passage beyond. She looked out of the window through its rain-spattered pane. Though it was dark and raining, she could see that water had flowing past their house and all the nearby ones. Its level, low right now, was rising every minute.

Already the water in the house was knee-deep, not ankle-deep. But how? She shook Mita out of her sleep. When she realized the situation, she screamed, "*Baan*(flood)! The Jaltungi is in flood!"

"But even then the water cannot be this high!" said Ratna even as they came out of the other door and clambered down the dark stairs. The water was now flowing over those stairs too – from Ratna's room that is, coming through the underground passage and flowing from the inside rather than from the outside. How was that possible?

Their screams had woken others up and all of them had gathered in the living room. Dishevelled and drowsy, they took in the situation.

"The rain has caused the Jaltungi river to flood and the pond to overflow," Neel reasoned, "Maybe because we cleared the pond, its internal link with the river has been activated."

"Yes," Jetha said, "And now that the mouth of the tunnel has got widened, the water has rushed in through it to Ratna's room, and then flowed down the staircase."

The water was indeed flowing down the stairs and falling into the living room where the water level was rising. Jethi-ma raised her sari up a little. It was getting wet and muddy at the border below.

"Come, we must leave," cried Mita. "But what about Kusum-dida? We can't leave her here !" said Ratna. Mita's mother came out of the small front room, holding Kusum-dida.

"I'll carry her out on my shoulder," Neel said.

All of them gathered whatever they could, a few essentials, money, identity and other cards.

"Don't forget the bag of Dokra crafts," Julian cried.

"Dokra craft!" cried Jetha as though Ratna was out of her senses.

Ratna picked it up and slung it over her shoulder on to her back.

Then they went `Splotch! Splotch!' up to the front door and opened it.

Immediately the water surged in from outside.

The distant river had come to their doorstep and was flowing through the village road. It was raining heavily as well.

Cries could be heard from the entire neighbourhood. The single street-light enabled Mita to see that everyone was out, trying to save themselves. Some were climbing up roof-tops, some were getting on to trees.

Branches and leaves, pots and pans, even boxes and tins were floating past in the swift current. The local strays were paddling valiantly.

"Get back!" cried Jetha "Neel, get back with Kusum-didi!" He shoved everybody back and slammed the front door shut. But it was too late for Ratna and Mita.

In the darkness and the rain, they had lost their footholds. The river water was carrying them away –in different directions.

Ratna could not make out anything more. She must have reached a fork in the road along which the river water was flowing. She saw Mita being swept inwards, past the mansion and the *kachhari* towards the interior of the village and Mita's own home. She felt herself being swept outwards, towards the fields, the railway station and the river beyond–she herself and the bag on her back.

And all this while, the rain came down incessantly.

38

In the Open Waters, Alone

The paddy fields were half-submerged by the dark flow. Ratna tried to clutch at the few shrubs that reared their heads but the current was too strong. She heard splashing and panting beside her. Two yellow eyes, a snout and bare fangs – it was the village stray trying to do his dog-strokes. Dida's Bhulo? A clump of bamboo – something hanging down from it – a snake – trying to snipe at the dog.

There was a tall electricity post ahead, a broken wire hanging low and giving out sparks. A live wire! What if the flow carried her to it and she got electrocuted?

The thought made her fling her arms and thrash her legs about – in an attempt to swim away from the post looming ahead.

The bag on her back slipped from her shoulder.

Ratna saw it fall and gave a half-scream. She lunged after it.

She even touched the strap, but could not really grasp it and it floated further away. It was heavy and dipped down in a matter of seconds.

Desperate, Ratna screamed. But in that wind and rain and thunder, who would hear that scream except herself?

The family jewels, hidden so cleverly by the last landlord – floating away!

After being safe from the coveted eyes of the greedy for decades and just been discovered by the new generation!

Ratna raised her head to the sky and screamed–like the howling foxes she had sometimes heard from woods beyond river Jaltungi.

There was a crackle of electricity from the broken wire atop the electric post.

Or was it a flash of lightning?

Ratna suddenly saw two arms arise from the water around the spot where the bag had sunk. Two arms that held the bag up.

Just then another pair of arms arose and snatched the bag away.

A third pair snatched it away for itself. A fourth pair arose. A fifth!

Ratna forgot to howl as she got carried away by the current beyond where the arms seemed to be playing a bizarre kind of water polo with the bag.

Aha, they were trying to keep it above the water level! Trying to save it from sinking!

But who were `they'?

Now they were flinging it high – high and still higher.

It was disappearing from sight.

Lost from sight. Lost.

Ratna could not see any more,

She floated away in a sort of daze, away and away till she hit something and stopped.

39

On the Railway Platform

A light shone upon her face. Ratna opened her eyes, she felt blood dripping from her forehead.

She realized that she had floated all the way down to the railway station. It had a raised platform and that was the level to which the river water had come up. Further, where the bare tracks lay, everything was under water. But the platform, though wet, was still slightly above the water. The stationmaster was also there, along with the guard. They would have gone in the late evening but it had started to rain heavily by then, and they had not been able to do that. The night staff had not been able to come either.

So, when Ratna came floating there and stopped on hitting the platform, she was spotted immediately, hauled up and provided first aid.

"This is the girl who had come that day! With two others!" exclaimed the station-master. "I know where she is from!" He used the railway telephonic equipment to send a message immediately to the old landline telephone at the mansion. In spite of the storm and the rain, the telephone lines were working. Soon there were reassuring voices from the other end. Everyone was safe.

The force of the rain had lessened by now, and the speed of the floodwater. The sky too seemed a little lighter. Was it getting to be morning?

The guard made some tea for Ratna. The hot beverage coursed through her veins. Her body was aching but, more than that, her heart was breaking.

To have lost the bag thus! How could she ever forgive herself! And what was that uncanny vision of hands popping out of the waters and playing with the bag? Had she passed out? Can you faint and yet float along?

Red streaks on the east. The torrents reduced to a faint drizzle. The water level seemed down an inch.

The electric pole gleamed pale in the early dawn. On top of it – as if flung there by invisible hands – hung the bag.

On the broken wire –as if it had been borne down by the wind and got pinned there–fluttered a scrap of paper.

“Get them down! Please don’t let them fly away again!” Ratna’s cries were frantic.

The guard waded through the water with a ladder kept at the station. He climbed and brought down the bag as well as the torn piece of paper. Although dripping wet, the Dokra artefacts were still there. Ratna opened the zip and checked. The paper too was wet and the writings on it had got smudged. But they could still be deciphered.

Matir bhitor ratan anek bhawra

Shakto holo segulo bar kawra.

Sonadana hiremanik jwale

Rukkho mati jodi bhasao jale.

It was the whole of the poem that Suresh Chowdhuri had remembered only in parts.

Matir bhitor ratan anek and *jodi bhasao jale.*

It was Ramesh Chowdhuri's last message that had been lost.

The rain had slowed down. The water was receding. A fresh layer of silt covered the fields. The paddy stalks were fresh and washed. So were the tomatoes and coriander in Neel-dada's organic farming area. The sun shone on all of them – bringing out the yellow and green and red – the gold, the emeralds and the rubies – in them.

"I know now what Ramesh Chowdhuri had really wanted to say!" Ratna cried out.

40

United with the Others

Hours later, Neel somehow managed to drive the car through the mud and reach the station.

The two of them hugged each other close in the utter relief of finding each other. "Mita? Dida? Binu? How are they?" asked Ratna through her sobs.

"Dida is much better! She still has a lot of life left in her. As for Mita, she has had some adventures. She had floated away in the direction opposite to you, trying to hold on to this and that. She had called out to Bhupen-kaka as she neared her house, and he had come out in the rain.

There was a mango tree near their house. Even in the dark, they could make out its outlines and they half-waded half-swam towards it. Bhupen helped Mita up first and clambered on to a branch himself. He tied Mita to the tree with a *gamchha* (thin local towel or wipe) he happened to be carrying.

But he had nothing to tie himself up with and so he merely clutched on to the tree.

By then the village had been flooded entirely. The river was sweeping across it. Utensils and boxes were floating out of houses and yards.

Mita saw something come floating out of their backyard, bobbing up and down. It was the plastic container of pesticide. It had been lying in their backyard. The floodwater had dislodged it and brought it out. As it was almost empty and tightly capped–it was bobbing up and down, not sinking. Then it suddenly got stuck in the lower branches of the mango tree that they were upon.

Somehow just then Bhupen-kaka lost his foothold and slipped from the tree. The current began to carry him away and Mita knew he did not know how to swim.

She wanted to jump and go after him. But she was tightly secured to the tree.

The pesticide container had by then come close to the mango tree.

So Mita bent and pushed it towards Bhupen-kaka – somehow.

"Catch it, Baba, and hang on to it," she called out and Bhupen-kaka did so. He held it to his chest and used it to keep himself afloat even as the current swept him away from the mango tree and the village.

"Then?" asked Ratna

"Well, then the day dawned, and the force of the waters became less, some villagers heard Mita's screams, untied her, and got her down from the tree. Sending her to us, they went looking for Bhupen-kaka. They found him, unconscious but alive, on a mound of bricks further down the village. The pesticide container had kept him bobbing up and down with itself till he had reached that high level. He lay on the bricks, the container still clutched to his chest.

But soon he recovered enough to go home with a few utensils and stuff that had flown out of his backyard, including the pesticide container that had saved his life.

As for Binu, he was safe and sound because he had been away at Prasad Karmakar's workshop at the time of the deluge, and the flood had not reached there. By now the car had come close to the mansion. Ratna was aghast at what she saw.

The provision shop was almost empty as it been open when the rains had started, and its packets and tins and boxes had floated away. Moti was trying to find them while Vishnu Poddar sat in the shop, clutching his hair in anguish.

The pond had no separate shape of its own. It had merged with the floodwater. The old palanquin had moved away from its place and was stuck at the bottom of the trees by the pond.

The mouth of the tunnel was utterly invisible under a sheet of water. It is through the tunnel through which water must have flowed, flooding the godown and then pouring into Ratna's bedroom. But there was no sign of the tunnel from above. Broken bricks and debris cluttered the entrance to the mansion and the almost swept-away Puja pavilion. But what was most devastating was the *baar mahal* wing. Water must have flown into it through the underground passage leading to the trap-door into which Ratna had fallen. It had ruined the *kachhari* from inside and made its walls collapse from the base. Gone was the seat of feudal power – the court where Ramesh Chowdhuri and his predecessors lorded over the likes of Gupi Mohan and Razak Mian.

In comparison, the *andar-mahal* was less affected. The inner apartments and the kitchen area had stood their ground. Ratna was smothered in welcome embraces from everybody – not just Baba and Ma.

41

The Message – Reviewed and Revealed

Jethi-ma, with the help of Khiri, was able to light a fire and cook a meal in the still-damp kitchen. In Mita's house, the kitchen was all but swept away. Besides, Dida still needed Mita's Ma to take care of her.

So, everybody sat to eat together, not on the floor, of course, which was still sopping wet. But here and there, wherever it was dry.

"*Luchi alur -dam*!" Jethi-ma announced, bringing them hot puffed-up puris and potato curry.

"How sweet they taste," said Mita. "Especially", said Bhupen-kaka, "after the fight with the elements last night."

"Yes," said his wife, "For this time we have fought to live instead of trying to die."

"What is more," laughed Baba, "this time you have fought back with that very pesticide container you tried to kill yourselves with!"

"Mita", said Bhupen-kaka, " we will never again give up the fight and leave you alone in the world."

"I will finally be able to have unbroken sleep," thought Mita.

"Bhupen-kaka," said Neel-dada, "Also promise never to use chemical pesticides. Turn organic, like me."

'Not again a lecture on organic farming!' thought Ratna. Surely, there is a time for everything?

She quickly said to Mita: "Let us cut off the top of that container, fill it up with earth, plant some flowering shrubs in it, and water it", she said. "It will bring out the real gems under the earth."

"Why, what do you mean?"

And then Ratna told them about what she thought Ramesh Chowdhuri, the last *jomidar* of Shalboni, had really wanted to tell his son Suresh:

Matir bhitor ratan anek bhawra

Shakto holo segulo bar kawra.

Sonadana hiremanik jwale

Rukkho mati jodi bhasao jale.

Inside, the earth is packed with jewel and gem

But it is tough to get your hands on them.

Gold and diamonds and rubies grow

If on dry earth you let water flow.

Ailing in last years, expecting the *jomidari* to be gone any day, Ramesh Chowdhuri had reached a philosophical view. Although he had packed some jewels within the Dokra artefacts, that is the limited and mundane interpretation of the above lines. That is not his real legacy. What he wanted to pass on to his sons and grandsons was the message that even when land reforms had taken away their status as landlords, they could still cultivate it and make the land yield its riches – food crops, fruits, and vegetables. It was the ripening paddy crops that were the real gold; the grains of rice, the pearls. Green vegetables like peas were the emeralds, fruits like the pomegranates the rubies, and so on. They were the actual treasures to be extracted out of the earth by irrigation and cultivation.

"Ah, I know a Hindi song which says the same," and Julian sang out: "*Meri desh ki dharti sona ugle ugle hire moti* (My motherland gives birth to gold and diamonds and pearls)."

"Perhaps you are right," Jetha said, "I never thought of it like that." Everybody nodded, looking serious.

"And my grandfather stole that paper," Kusum-dida spoke out, "thinking that it contains clues that would make him rich! And I clung to his papers thinking that someday I might find it among them."

"Why, Dida, how did you know that he had stolen it?"

Ratna remembered what she had seen in the *kachhari*. "He told me on his deathbed", said Dida, "But, Ratna, how did you get hold of that scrap of paper?"

"Where did you find it?" asked Neel.

"Tell us immediately," ordered Jethi-ma. "Not just about the paper but also about the bag."

"You won't believe me when I tell you," replied Ratna.

But she told them. She recounted all her strange experiences, ending with the one last night.

Outside the rain had almost stopped and faint sunlight could be seen. The flow of water had slowed down. A few villagers had ventured out. A dog was barking.

“Whose arms do you think they were?” asked Baba after a while.

“Som, how can you ask such a question!” Jetha reproached him but went on to say: “Of course, they were her delusions. Anyway, answer him!”

“I don’t have an answer,” Ratna said. “There were four pairs of hands Ramesh Chowdhuri, Jishnu *mahajan*, Haru *lathiyal*, Shyamu – I think they were all there. All four had had some links with it. But I like to think that it was Ramesh Chowdhuri who had flung it up on the electric post. It was his legacy and he wanted it to reach us.”

“Absurd!” snorted Jetha. “Ghosts and spirits do not exist. They just do not.”

“It could also have been my father, trying to atone!” said Kusum-dida.

“Nonsense!” said Jetha again.

CHAPTER 10

42

The Message - No Longer Lost

Two years later.

Ratna was once again at Shalboni with her parents. She gazed adoringly at the green expanse of fields and fruit trees, the modernized local hospital, and the renovated Chowdhuri Niwas. The provision store too had been rebuilt. The village was cleaner and the pond, a clear blue. Dwijesh Chowdhuri and Somesh Chowdhuri had come into much wealth from the sale of family jewels that the X-rays revealed to be hidden within the Dokra artefacts. But, with the happy consent of their wives, they had used it for rural development. The flooding of Jaltungi had covered the parched land with silt and made it more fertile. Agriculture in and around Shalboni had got a fresh lease of life. Neel, in collaboration with Julian and Tessa, had successfully cultivated organic vegetables. Other farmers too, Bhupen-kaka a leading figure among them, were taking it up or at least being judicious in the use of chemical fertilizers and pesticides. Kusum-dida's garden too had gone organic and was fetching her a good bit of money. As part of the general prosperity, the Dokra workshop of Shalboni was also flourishing, getting more and more publicity. Only,

Vishnu Poddar had sold his store and shifted his business to a distant village, even beyond Amodpur.

Ratna looked happily all around, with Neel, Julian, Tessa, and Mita by her side. "Wouldn't Ramesh Chowdhuri be happy to see all this!" she said and recited his lines once more.

Inside, the earth is packed with jewel and gem

But it is tough to get your hands on them.

Gold and diamonds and rubies grow

If on dry earth you let water flow.

Well, the emeralds, rubies and gold are out there all around us. His last message is not lost."

"Yes," said Julian, "even though Suresh Chowdhuri, his son, lost it, he recovered it through to his great-granddaughter Ratna and great-grandson Neelesh," Julian said.

Neel suddenly looked a bit sulky. "I don't see why he had to wait all that long to arrange ghostly theatres for Ratna in the *kachhari* or water polo games in floodwater. He could have told me! I have often gone to the *kachhari* and the railway station. Why didn't I ever see or sense anything!"

"Perhaps," said Tessa, her nose-ring catching the sunlight, "perhaps because your mind was already crammed with ideas and information and history. Ratna's mind was clean and fresh – with more space on it to absorb signals from the spirits."

"Perhaps he was scared that you would start to lecture him", said Julian, "and never stop."

"Yes," said Neel. "Who knows when the past overflows into the present, like floodwater carrying debris from afar, and upsetting the order of time."

"Who knows," said Mita dreamily.

Ratna drew in the air that blew over the fields and smiled, saying:

"The last message is no longer a lost message!"

***

Glossary

A

Ada: ginger, adrak

Aam: mango

Amodpur: a village near Bengal-Bihar border

Akhrha: place of performance, arena, akhada,

Alkhallas: flowing robes of Bauls

Andar mahal: inner apartments

B

Baan: flood

Babu: epithet of Bengali gentry

Baar mahal: outer apartments

Bari: house

Baul: wandering folk-singers of Bengal

Bhulo: name of a village dog

Binu: name of a village lad

C

Chirasthayi Bandovast: Permanent Settlement 1793

Chowdhuri: a Bengali surname, typical of the landed gentry

D

Dada: elder brother

Daag: marking of Plot Number in Field Index register at district records office

Daktar: doctor

Damodar: a flood-prone river of Bengal and Bihar

Dida: grandmother, Dadi

Didi: elder sister

Dokra: an artistic metal-craft

Dwijesh (Chowdhuri): grandson of Ramesh Chowdhuri, elder son of Suresh Chowdhuri, father of Neelesh or Neel

E

Ektara: single-string harp-type musical instrument of Bauls

G

Gamchha: thin local towel

H

Halud: turmeric, haldi

Haru: name of a guard of landlord Ramesh Chowdhuri

J

Jalkhabar: puffed-up *puri*s o fl our se rved wi th ried slices of brinjal or potato.

Jaltungi: a small river flowing into the Damodar

Jaam: jamun

Jhola: shoulder-bag

Jomi: land

Jomidar: landlord in pre-independence India

Jomidar-bari: zamindar's haveli, landlord's mansion

Jetha: uncle, father's elder brother

Jethi-ma: aunty, wife of Jetha

K

Kachhari: court, office

Kachuri-pana: water hyacinth

Kajal: kohl

Kaka: father's younger brother or someone in that position

Kantthal: jackfruit

Karmakar: blacksmith, also a surname for blacksmiths

Khata: exercise book

Khiri: name of a maid of the Chowdhuris

Kolkhozy: collective farm, of USSR

Kurta: half-shirt

L

Lathiyal: guards wielding lathi or sticks

Luchi alur-dam: pu ed-up puri with spicy potato curry

M

Moshai: colloquial form of mahashay, a man of respect

Mati: earth, clay

Mahajan: moneylender, small businessman

Mita: name of a Bengali girl, meaning `a friend'

Mohur: gold coin

N

Namaskar: Bengali gesture of respectful greeting

Niwas: abode, mansion

Neelesh: a name referring to the blue gem Neela

P

Pajama: ethnic form of pants

Palki: palanquin of old times

Panna: emerald

Patthshala: village primary school

Papaya: a juicy fruit

Peepul: Peepal tree

Poddar: a Bengali surname

R

Ramesh (Chowdhuri): deceased old zamindar of Shalboni village area

Ratan: gem

Ratna: a Bengali girl's name, meaning gem

S

Saag: herbs, green vegetables

Salwar-kameez: typical dress-suit of north India

Sandesh: Bengali sweetmeat

Shalboni: a village on the Bengal-Bihar border

Shyamu: name of a boy

Somesh (Chowdhuri): grandson of Ramesh Chowdhuri, younger son of Suresh Chowdhuri, father of Ratna

Sovkhozy: collective farm of USSR

T

Taka: money

Thakur-dalan: pavilion for puja ceremonies

Thakur-po: younger brother in law